Delete

Confidentially
YOURS

Brooke's Bad Luck

5

ALSO BY JO WHITTEMORE

JO WHITTEMORE

Confidentially

YOURS

Brooke's Bad Luck

HARPER

An Imprint of HarperCollinsPublishers

Library of Congress Control Number: 2016944448
ISBN 978-0-06-235901-8

Typography by Kate J. Engbring
16 17 18 19 20   OPM   10 9 8 7 6 5 4 3 2 1
❖
First Edition

To you, the reader!
Thank you for sharing in the adventures of
Brooke, Vanessa, Heather, and Tim!

Contents

1

The Woman in the Cottage

I t was a dark and stormy night . . .

Actually, it was a cold and snowy day, but no scary adventure ever starts like that. Unless there's a killer snowman. And even *that's* only scary until someone throws hot cocoa at him.

Anyway, why was I hoping for horror? Because so far my winter break had been dull with a capital ZZZZ. You'd think life in the Chicago suburbs would give me tons of stories to tell, but my most exciting news was Hammie and Chelsea, my cats, playing hide-and-seek in the Christmas tree.

Pine tree peekaboo: the highlight of my break.

Meanwhile my friends had awesome stories from their winter vacations. Heather Schwartz, one of my BFFs, had been in the spotlight on a holiday parade float with her choir, and Vanessa Jackson, my other bestie, had gone to Disney World with her brother and mom.

But I was probably most jealous of my friend Tim Antonides.

Not long ago, Tim became buddies with Berkeley Dennis, one of the richest and coolest kids at Abraham Lincoln Middle School. That alone wasn't very exciting, but Berkeley's cousin happened to be motocross superstar Adrenaline Dennis! He came to town for the holidays and took Berkeley and Tim to watch him practice for the X Games.

Heather and Vanessa couldn't have cared less when Tim bragged about going, but I was super jealous. I like sports just as much as he does. In fact, I give sports advice for Lincoln's Letters, the advice column at the *Lincoln Log*, my school newspaper. *Plus*, I'm captain of my soccer team, the Berryville Strikers. But I didn't even bother asking Tim if he could score me an invite. I got a major dudes-only vibe from the whole thing . . . mainly because Tim said, "It'll be dudes only."

So when another friend, Katie Kestler, asked if I wanted to visit a fortune-teller with her the day before spring semester, I instantly said, "Yes! Please! I'm about to start dressing up the cats!"

It was easy to talk Vanessa into coming since she's usually up for anything, but Heather was a little harder to convince. In fact, she still had doubts after Katie's mom, Bobbi, parked in front of a cottage with a wooden sign that read, "Madame Delphi: Seer Extraordinaire."

"Are we sure this is a good idea?" asked Heather, eyeing some gargoyles on either side of the front door. "I mean . . . what if we accidentally summon an evil spirit or something?"

"Don't worry. Madame Delphi's a professional who can handle anything," said Bobbi. "And I'll be right here waiting, so you can run out any time."

Heather didn't look reassured but opened the car door anyway.

"Tell Madame I said hi!" Bobbi called as my friends and I got out. "And that she was right about avoiding the salmon!"

I glanced back as Katie closed the car door and waved to her mom. "Why isn't she coming with us?" I asked.

"Bobbi has to make a conference call," said Katie, "and Madame Delphi only likes disembodied voices that come from spirits."

Heather spun toward us, nostrils flared. "So there *are* going to be ghosts?"

"Of course not," said V, putting a hand on her arm.

"But if there were, that would be awesome!" I charged through the snow and up the front steps, each plank of wood squeaking under my weight. "This place is creepy!"

"That's what bothers me." Heather shivered in her puffy green coat.

"Oh come on," Katie coaxed, putting an arm through one of Heather's. "It's a new year. Don't you want to know what's going to happen?"

I knocked on the front door, which opened by itself.

Heather turned to Katie. "Will I even live to see it?"

Vanessa stepped up to Heather's other side. "Don't worry, we'll be right here with you. The whole time."

Then V slipped and fell on her butt.

I cringed, Katie and Heather gasped, but Vanessa lay back in the snow and laughed.

Even when she's down, she's smiling.

"How the heck did that happen?" I asked while Katie and Heather helped her up. "The snow isn't slippery."

"No, but the bottoms of my boots are." V lifted a foot just high enough for us to see that the sole was worn smooth.

"Hmm. Time to trash those," said Heather.

Vanessa and Katie screeched in horror.

"Are you insane?" asked Katie.

"They're vintage Dior!" added Vanessa.

The two of them are a little crazy for clothes. They're working on their own designer label, KV Fashions, and Vanessa offers style advice for Lincoln's Letters.

That's right; Vanessa writes the column, too, along with Heather and Tim! V, Heather, and I actually came up with the idea, since we'd been giving one another advice for years. Vanessa answers questions about beauty and fashion, I handle sports and fitness, Tim contributes the guy's point of view, and Heather fixes friendships and relationships because she has a way with people.

Like right now.

Instead of rolling her eyes, which was what I was doing, Heather said, "You know, if those boots are special, you might want to wait and wear them in the spring. Otherwise the water from the snow could wreck them."

Vanessa eyes widened, and she lifted one foot off the ground, balancing precariously on the other like a fashionable flamingo.

"Oh for crying out loud," I said, leaping off the porch and running over to her. Unlike my glamorous friend, I was wearing appropriate winter clothes: real snow boots, jeans, and a thermal jacket. I turned my back to Vanessa and crouched to give her a piggyback ride. "Come on, V. The future awaits!"

She laughed and climbed on. "Don't drop me!" she warned.

I trudged up the steps with her, Heather hesitantly followed, and Katie ran ahead to push the door open the rest of the way.

Instead of the usual chimes to announce visitors, a harp strummed, giving our entrance a mystical feel. Goose bumps covered my arms, despite the fact that I was wearing a coat *and* a Vanessa. She slid off my back, boots thumping on the wooden floor, and said, "Whoa, check this place out!"

It took my eyes a minute to adjust to the darkened room. At one point it'd probably been several rooms, but the dividing walls had been knocked out and just a few support columns remained. The windows were covered with heavy velvet curtains, and the only light came from flickering oil lamps attached to the walls.

"This place is straight out of a movie," I murmured. "I love it."

"Can we please get this over with?" asked Heather, standing as close to the front door as she could without physically being a part of it.

"My mom says Madame usually has people wait in either the sitting area or gift shop," said Katie. "So I think she'll come get us when she's ready."

"Ooh." I rubbed my hands together excitedly. "How will she know we're here? Will a spirit from the beyond tell her?"

"More like a security camera from the ceiling," said V, pointing at an orb mounted above us.

"Aww." I lowered my hands.

Katie grinned at me. "Just pretend it's an all-seeing eye," she said in a spooky voice.

I snickered and glanced around. The sitting area to our left was decorated with a dumpy couch and chairs that had cracked seat cushions. The gift shop area was to the right and crowded with tables and bookshelves and spinning racks, all filled with various mystical items sporting orange price stickers.

Needless to say, my friends and I were drawn to the right.

"What is all this stuff?" asked V, pulling a book titled *Blessings and Curses* from a shelf. She flipped to a random page. " 'Give your enemy bad breath.' "

"How?" asked Heather, reading over her shoulder.

"Easy. Garlic." I ran my finger over the spines of the other books. "I wonder if Tim's read any of these."

He was obsessed with books, particularly the classics. Although something told me *Crockpot Love Potions* probably wasn't on his list.

I moved on to a table covered with boxes of

candles, packets of herbs, and little knickknacks. "Hey, anybody wanna play poker?" I asked, plucking a deck of cards from the pile.

Katie laughed. "Good luck with that. Those are tarot cards."

"Tarot cards?" I slid a couple out of the box. One of them had a guy in a jester's costume and was labeled "The Fool." The other, "The Tower," was just that: an image of a tower. "What is it, a matching game?"

She shook her head. "They're for telling fortunes."

I put the cards back and picked up a pocket-size horseshoe. "I'd like to see the horse who can wear this."

Somewhere behind us hinges creaked, and we all turned toward the sound. A tall, blond woman in a flowing purple dress shuffled in our direction from an open door between the oil lamps.

"Good afternoon. I am Madame Delphi," she said with a slight bow and a breathy voice. "I understand you wish to see the future."

"I actually wish to see a mirror," said V, wrapping a silky scarf around her neck. "Also, do you have this in blue?"

Heather elbowed her in the side, and Madame Delphi raised an eyebrow.

"Everything in the shop is as-is," she said. "Including my predictions." She pressed her fingertips together. "I must warn you that people can be disappointed by what I see. They beg for a different future." She shook her head, eyes locked on mine. "But your future will be what it will be."

Again, goose bumps.

"Now," she said in a soft voice, "who will go first?"

Katie hurried to the front as if Madame Delphi was handing out designer dresses. "Hi! I'm Katie

Kestler and you did a reading for my mom, Bobbi Kestler, and you told her to skip the salmon at a wedding and she did and everyone who ate it got food poisoning, but not her because she didn't eat it." Katie paused for oxygen. "So she said to tell you that you were right, and I am more than ready to have my fortune read!" She turned to the rest of us. "I mean . . . if that's okay."

V and I nodded.

"You can go for me, too," said Heather.

Madame Delphi arched a brow. "You fear the future?"

"No." Heather shrank back. "I fear this moment right now."

"Aww." I put an arm around her. "Heather, you don't have to go in if you don't want."

"Yeah." V bumped her. "We just thought this would be fun to do together."

"Well . . . I want to have fun," Heather said, nodding toward the door Madame Delphi had come through. "Is it even darker in there?"

Madame Delphi approached Heather and took her hands. "Let me make this easy. It won't be as accurate but . . ." She flipped Heather's hands to face palms up. "Are you left- or right-handed?"

"Left," said Heather, glancing curiously from her hands to Madame Delphi.

Madame Delphi studied Heather's palms for a moment and smiled. "My, you are a talent, aren't you?"

"She's an *amazing* singer," I chimed in.

Heather smiled and blushed. "I'm okay."

"Your talent will take you far," said Madame Delphi, tracing a finger along Heather's palm. "And you will live a long, happy life." She rested a hand on each of Heather's and stepped away. "There now. Was that so terrible?"

"Not at all," said Heather, beaming.

Katie scooted closer. "Is it my turn?"

Madame Delphi nodded. "Would you like—"

"The works!" exclaimed Katie, already bounding toward the open door.

Five minutes later Katie bounded back out to the sitting area where Heather, V, and I were waiting.

"Next!" she chirped.

"I'm guessing you got a good fortune?" I asked, looking up from the pack of tarot cards I was building into a house.

"Oh, not just me," said Katie. She flopped onto a couch next to Vanessa and raised a cloud of dust in the process. "Vanny too!"

Vanessa lowered the copy of *Natural Beauty* she was reading. "Your fortune included me?"

"Well . . . KV Fashions," Katie explained. She rubbed the thumb and fingertips of one hand together. "Madame Delphi said money's gonna flow like a river!" She nudged V. "Ask Madame Delphi about money, but don't tell her we work together. I guarantee she'll say we make more this year."

"Of course we will," said V with a smirk. "We can't possibly make less than last year's nothing."

We all laughed.

So far KV Fashions' only big business project had been makeovers for the Fall Into Winter dance, and the price had been a clothing item for charity. It was a sweet gesture, but afterward, V told me they'd given up about twenty-five bucks each in the process.

"Go on." Katie prodded V. "And try to get details, like what specifically makes us richety-rich." Her eyes sparkled.

V glanced down at where I was sitting on the floor. "Would it be okay if I went next? The future of KV Fashions may or may not be riding on this." She leaned closer. "I'm betting on 'not.'"

"I can hear you!" said Katie from over her shoulder.

"Sure," I said with a nod. "I've got the second story of my card house to work on anyway."

While V walked off to meet Madame Delphi, Heather moved from one of the cracked chairs to sit next to Katie on the couch.

"What else did she tell you?" asked Heather.

"Yeah, did you ask when you were going to die?" I chimed in.

Heather turned to me with wide eyes. "Brooke!"

"What? I'm going to ask when it's *my* turn. This woman can see the future! Why stop at 'Will I win the Women's World Cup?'"

Katie laughed. "It's fine. And no, I didn't ask because I already know I'm going to live to be super old. Everyone in my family does . . . except my great-grandpa Pete, who fell in a volcano."

Heather and I both raised our eyebrows.

"Okay, there's way more to *that* story," I said, putting down my cards.

When V emerged from the back room, it was to find me, Heather, and Katie laughing so hard we were crying. Even though she had no idea why, Vanessa joined in.

"Poor Pete," said Heather between giggles. "That banana sandwich just wasn't worth it."

We all calmed down, and I poked Vanessa in the side. "How was your time with the teller?"

"Fun!" she said. "We talked about fashion and Disney World."

Katie, Heather, and I looked at one another.

"What about your reading?" asked Katie.

"Well, I'm going to get less clumsy," she said, making a thumbs-up. "But she didn't mention anything about getting rich." She held up a finger. "Although there are about to be major changes in my love life."

"Ooh!" Heather rubbed her hands together. "Between you and Gil?"

Gil Pendleton was Vanessa's boyfriend, who

also happened to work at the *Lincoln Log* with us doing horoscopes and photography.

I narrowed my eyes in mock dismay. "V, I don't want to be on your reality show, *Middle School Marriage*."

Everyone started laughing again, including Vanessa, who placed her hands on her blushing cheeks.

"I could melt snow with my face right now!" she exclaimed.

Madame Delphi appeared in the doorway, and we quieted.

"We're so sorry!" said Katie. "We didn't mean to disturb the spirit world."

"It's all right. There was one more of you waiting to see me?" asked Madame Delphi.

"That's me!" I got to my feet and stepped over my tarot-card house.

Madame Delphi nodded and gestured for me to follow. I waved at my friends before stepping

108

through the doorway into a smaller, even darker room.

"Please sit," said Madame Delphi, pointing to a small table with two chairs across from each other. There wasn't a crystal ball like I'd been expecting. Just another pack of tarot cards and a tea set.

I scooted my chair as close to the table as possible and placed both hands in the center, palms up. Now for the real excitement!

"I won't be reading your palms today," said Madame Delphi. "It is a very inexact practice."

"Oh." I withdrew my hands.

Madame Delphi reached for the teapot and poured hot water into a cup, placing it in front of me. I peered inside and saw leaves skittering along the bottom.

"Let that sit for a few minutes while we turn the cards," she said.

She passed them to me and asked me to

shuffle. "I need the cards to pick up your energy and presence."

I looked down at the cards. "Um . . . okay."

When I was done, she had me spread the cards facedown across the table.

"Choose three," she said. "To represent your past, present, and future."

I selected three and handed them to her. As she turned them over, she explained what they meant.

"The Strength card reveals you have accomplished much."

I sat a little straighter in my chair and puffed out my chest. "Yep!"

"The Three of Pentacles means you are currently in a position where you must collaborate and work well with others."

"I'm the team leader for my advice column and captain of my soccer team," I said.

She nodded. "Your cards represent you well."

Madame Delphi flipped the last card and gasped.

"What?" I asked.

"Your future," she said, "is represented by the Nine of Swords!" In a softer voice she added, "The lord of cruelty."

That didn't sound promising.

"What . . . what does that mean?" I managed to squeak out.

"Great sorrow and grief," said Madame Delphi. She patted my hand. "Perhaps the tea will reveal something more." She pushed the cup closer to me. "Drink everything but the leaves."

I chugged the tea, even though it was still hot and kind of gross, hoping for a better fortune at the bottom of the cup.

Madame Delphi gave me more instructions on how to swirl the leaves around and focus my thoughts on a particular question.

"What's the source of my sorrow and grief?" I asked.

"Now let the leaves settle," she instructed me. "And tell me what you see."

I did as she said, holding the cup at arm's length so I could inspect it from every angle.

"It looks like a big O," I said.

Madame Delphi rubbed her chin. "Do you have any enemies whose names start or end with O?"

I shook my head. My soccer archrival was Lacey Black, and my only enemy from school was a kid named Ryan Durstwich.

"Do you have any issues with foods that start with O?"

I shook my head again. "Although one time I ate an Oreo that my friend Tim had sitting at the bottom of his backpack."

Madame Delphi wrinkled her nose but

continued. "Do you see *anything* else in the cup?"

I lifted it again. "Just my reflection."

"Hmm." Madame Delphi pressed her fingertips together and studied me. "Perhaps that is not an *O* in your cup but a mirror."

"A mirror?" My forehead wrinkled for a second, and then my mouth dropped open. "You think *I'm* the source of my sorrow?"

"We are our own worst enemies," said Madame Delphi with a solemn nod. She held out a hand to me. "Please give me the palm of your nondominant hand."

I held out my left, and she pressed her fingers into the lines, muttering to herself.

"What? What do you see?" I asked in a mildly panicked voice.

"Your hands are incredibly dirty." She withdrew her fingers and wiped them on her skirt. "But the good news is you have a very long life line. Whatever tragedy befalls you will not kill you."

I swallowed hard and brought my hands to my chest. "And the bad news?"

Madame Delphi sighed and fixed her eyes on mine. "You're in for a great deal of bad luck."

CHAPTER

2

Trading Places

"That'll be ten dollars."

I was back in the front room with my friends, and Madame Delphi was behind the register, collecting her fortune for telling ours.

With a sour smile I handed over the money while my friends chatted.

"Would you like a receipt?" asked Madame Delphi.

"I'd like a better fortune," I replied, but she just smiled and shrugged.

"As I said before, I cannot change your future. I can only tell you what it will be."

She bade us farewell and approached a woman sitting on the waiting-area couch.

"You must be Alice," I heard her say.

"Hey, Brooke?" Katie tapped my shoulder. "Ready to go?"

I nodded and followed her and the rest of my friends toward the exit.

"You never told us what your fortune was," Vanessa commented, opening the front door. "Are you going to be rich? Famous?"

I sighed. "Doomed, according to Madame Delphi."

My friends stopped in the doorway and stared at me. Icy wind brought snowflakes inside to melt at our feet.

"Girls, in or out, please," Madame Delphi called.

I nudged my friends out the door and closed it behind us.

"She didn't actually say 'doomed,' did she?"

asked V. She started down the steps, leaving room for me to walk beside her, but I took my time. If bad luck was coming, I wasn't taking any chances.

"Not that exact word," I said. "But when we did tarot cards, I drew the Nine of Swords."

Katie gasped and threw her arms around me. "Oh, sweetie, I'm so sorry!"

V and Heather exchanged curious looks.

"What does that mean?" asked Heather.

"Yeah, the more swords the better, right?" added V.

Katie shook her head. "The Nine of Swords is bad. Very bad." She opened the passenger side door of Bobbi's car. "Brooke drew the Nine of Swords."

Bobbi's face paled a little, and she patted the front passenger seat. "Brooke, you'll sit up here. It's got the best air bags."

The blood must have left my face, because

Vanessa made a scoffing sound and squeezed my shoulder. "Nothing's going to happen," she said. "If anyone was going to pull that card, it should've been me."

"Yeah," said Heather. "There's no such thing as bad luck."

I raised an eyebrow. "At your Halloween party you wouldn't let a girl dressed as a black cat cross your path."

"That was different." She blushed. "I was carrying nachos and didn't want to bump into her. You know how important junk food is to me."

Junk food, health food . . . it all mattered to Heather. She had a bottomless stomach. Or a tapeworm.

"Vanessa's right. It's probably nothing," said Katie.

"Honey . . . ," her mom intoned.

Katie leaned into the car and whispered loudly, "Look, I know she's in trouble, and *you* know she's in trouble, but I can at least try to make her feel better!" She turned sideways and smiled at me. "Everything's going to be a-okay!"

I rolled my eyes. "Thanks for the pep talk."

She stepped back so I could get in the front seat, and Bobbi gave me a pitying smile.

I cleared my throat. "So Katie says she's going to make a lot of money this year!"

Bobbi beamed at her daughter in the rear-view mirror. "Tell me everything."

After Katie told her mom her fortune, Vanessa and Heather gave theirs. Nobody asked for details about mine, and I was happy to stay quiet.

When the SUV stopped in front of my house, I thanked Bobbi for the ride and said good-bye to my friends. V rolled down her window to call out, "Everything's going to be fine!"

I nodded and trudged up the front walk and into the house. Hammie loped to the door to greet me with Chelsea scurrying behind on kitten paws.

"Hi, cuties." I bent and cuddled them while I took off my boots. They helped by chewing on the laces. In a louder voice, I shouted, "I'm home!"

Nobody answered, and I felt a teeny bit of worry creep up as I wandered the first floor with the cats at my heels. On a typical Sunday my folks would be in the living room watching TV until it was time for us to have dinner. But there wasn't so much as a dent in the couch cushions.

Suddenly, Mom shrieked from upstairs.

Chelsea and Hammie scattered, and I sprinted up the steps . . . alone . . . toward danger . . . failing Horror Movie 101.

"Mom!" I called.

I found both my parents in the office, sopping up coffee from a stack of papers. Dad was wearing his workout clothes, and in the corner the treadmill was whirring to a stop.

"Are you guys okay?" I asked. "Did Mom drop her coffee when she saw you working out?"

Both my parents laughed.

"We're fine," she said, shaking coffee off a page. "I just thought these W-2s could use a drink."

Mom's an accountant, which means after the new year she's really busy doing people's taxes. Dad works for an ad agency, and until recently he'd been a workaholic, spending a lot of time away from home. Then he saw I was kind of following in his footsteps and relaxed his routine.

"And I'm trying to keep a New Year's resolution, smarty-pants," said Dad. With a smirk, he added, "I'm surprised your fortune-teller didn't see that coming."

"Ugh." I flopped onto a chair. "She was too busy predicting my doom."

Mom snorted and regarded me with an amused smile. "Don't tell me you believe what she said." Mom wadded up a soiled towel and organized her papers.

"The cards and the tea leaves and my palm all agreed," I informed her.

Dad grabbed his gym towel and water bottle off the treadmill. "Well, we knew this day was coming. The seer at the fair warned us."

I sighed and stared at the ceiling. "Why do I tell you guys anything? This is serious!"

Dad nodded and stepped closer. "You're right. We need to bless you with holy water." He uncapped his squeeze bottle. "Ready?"

Mom squealed and crawled out of the way, and I just grinned at Dad. "You wouldn't dare."

"Oh, wouldn't I?" He grinned wickedly and squeezed the bottle. A stream of water shot out, and I slid off the chair and onto the floor, but

Dad redirected his aim and got me in the neck.

"Ahhh! It's so cold!" I shrieked, rolling away to escape it.

"I'm only doing this for your own good," he said. More water came rushing at me.

"Mom! Save me!" I called between giggles, reaching out for her.

"Aww, I'd like to, sweetie," she said with an apologetic shrug. "But if these documents get any wetter, they'll be papier-mâché."

Dad paused in his water-bottle assault. "Do you want me to stop?"

"Yes!" I laughed and pulled my hair back.

"Are you going to stop believing in bad luck?"

"Yes!"

Dad threw me his gym towel.

"Ew! It's damp!" I tossed it back and got to my feet. "I'm gonna dry off with a good towel. You two are so weird." I headed to the bathroom with Mom calling, "At least we're never boring!"

My parents told me a lot of things I didn't agree with (too much pizza would kill me, pizza wasn't a food group, the government was going to outlaw pizza), but as much as I hated to admit it, I had a feeling they were right about the luck thing. I didn't even pause when I tripped over the carpet.

Everyone pulled a Vanessa once in a while.

A typical wake-up for me used to be Hammie purring and rubbing against my arm. But the first morning back to school I woke up to Hammie's purrs *and* Chelsea's paw tapping on my nose.

"Silly thing!" I said with a giggle, nudging her aside. Unfortunately, I didn't realize she was at the edge of the bed, and Chelsea slipped over. "Chelsea!"

She fell with a mew, and I grabbed for her in midair as she grabbed for me.

The only difference was that she had claws.

There's nothing quite as painful as tiny needles ripping into flesh, and I couldn't help letting out a scream. In under a minute, both my parents were thundering up the stairs.

"Brooke? Are you okay?" called Mom.

They walked in to find Chelsea licking her paws while I cradled *my* bleeding paw.

"What happened?" asked Dad, inspecting it. "Did Chelsea do this?"

I nodded. "It was an accident. She was falling off the bed and I caught her."

Mom lifted Chelsea by the scruff of her neck and deposited her on the carpet. "Down you go, killer." She helped me out of bed as Dad continued to study the wounds.

"Is it really bad?" I asked. "Do I need stitches?"

He shook his head. "You might have some scarring, and we'll have to watch for cat scratch fever, but you should be fine."

"Cat scratch fever?" I narrowed my eyes.

"Are you messing with me?"

"Not this time," said Dad, crossing his heart. "We need to wash your scratches so they don't get infected. And don't let either of the cats lick your cuts."

I wrinkled my nose. "Wasn't planning on it."

Getting my hand cleaned and dressed with bandages put me behind schedule so that by the time I got to school, homeroom had already started. When I walked in, I gave Ms. Maxwell my note with my injured hand so she'd know it was serious.

"Oh my. Are you okay?" she asked, turning my hand over.

I nodded. "As long as the cat scratch fever doesn't set in."

Her forehead wrinkled in concern. "Well, let me know if you need to leave early to see the nurse."

I took my seat, and instantly Vanessa turned

to look at me. "What's with your hand? Did you step on it with a soccer cleat?"

"No," I said with a laugh. "How could someone step on their own hand?"

"It's been known to happen," she said with a serious expression, covering one of her hands with the other. "But for real, what's under the bandage?"

I told her about the daring midair rescue of Chelsea, and she winced.

"Ouch! Talk about bad luck," said V. Then her eyes widened. "Wait. I mean—"

"Of course!" I exclaimed.

"Ladies, keep it down, please," Ms. Maxwell warned.

I lowered my voice and leaned close to V. "It's just like the fortune-teller predicted!"

"It's nothing like the fortune-teller predicted," she whispered back. "She said you were in for some big tragedy, remember?" She smacked herself on the forehead. "Shoot! I mean—"

"You're right," I said in a soft voice. "Things are going to get worse. What's next? Am I going to be mauled by a mountain lion?"

My pen rolled off the desk, and I went to grab it at the same time as V. We knocked skulls, and I grimaced. "See? Bad luck!"

"This isn't bad luck," she said, rubbing her head. "This is a typical Monday for me!"

"Yeah, well, it's not for me," I said. "And I don't plan to make it a habit."

Apparently, the universe had something else in mind.

Later, as we were leaving homeroom, someone shouted, "Heads up!"

Normally, I'm fast enough to catch whatever's flying past, but that morning I turned and got nailed in the face with a highlighter.

"Owww!" I yelled, clutching my nose.

V pulled me to the side of the hall. "Is there blood? Can you breathe?"

I pulled my hand away, which thankfully was clean, and sniffed hard. "It's okay." My eyes lit up. "And I can smell pepperoni pizza!"

"See?" said V with a laugh. "Things are looking up already."

We walked into the main hall where my boyfriend, Abel, was waiting with his hands behind his back. Since he's a seventh grader, I normally only see him before school or between our lunches or classes.

"Okay, things are a little better," I agreed with V. She squeezed my arm, waved to Abel, and disappeared into the crowd.

"Hi!" He greeted me with a hug. "I didn't see you this morning, so I figured I'd check on the unluckiest girl in Berryville. How are you?"

I'd texted Abel after the trip to Madame

Delphi's and told him everything.

I smirked and held up my hand. "Two injuries and counting."

"Two?" he asked, looking me over.

"I got hit in the face with a highlighter," I explained.

"Well, on the bright side . . ." He paused and grinned. "Get it? Because it's a highlighter?"

I grinned too. "You're lucky I like you."

"I really am." He took my hand, and we walked down the hall. "And I got you something."

Abel held out what he'd been holding behind his back. "It's a four-leaf clover. I thought it might help."

Someone jostled past him, knocking the clover out of his palm. Before he could retrieve it, several other kids stepped on the clover until it was a green smudge in the carpet.

He and I both stared at the smudge.

"That seems about right," I said.

Abel sighed. "Bye, two bucks."

I squeezed him. "It's the thought that counts."

"You know you're not really unlucky, right?" he asked.

I took a deep breath and said, "Ask me again at the end of the day."

We parted ways at my math class, where I proceeded to get my pen jammed in the pencil sharpener.

"Why on earth were you trying to sharpen your pen?" asked my math teacher as the school maintenance guy fiddled with the machine.

"I was thinking about something else," I said. "I'm sorry."

"I'm sorry" became my motto, as I dropped my math book on someone's foot in the hallway after class, then tripped over two of my teammates in dodgeball and got us all tagged out.

"I promise I'm normally much better," I said

when they grumbled. "I could take on the entire class on a good day!"

When I sat down at lunch with Heather, Tim, and Vanessa, the first words out of my mouth were "I'm sorry."

Heather wrinkled her forehead. "For what? You just got here."

"Yes, but in the next thirty minutes, I will either spill or spit something onto each of you." I pointed at all of my friends.

"I don't like this lunch game," said Tim.

"It's not a game. She thinks she has bad luck," explained Vanessa.

"I don't think it. I know it," I informed her, filling them all in on my morning.

"Sounds like you and Vanessa switched bodies," said Tim with a smirk.

Vanessa stared at him. "Normally I'd hit you for that, but today *has* been a pretty good day for me. I only got my scarf caught in my locker once!" She beamed as if all her birthday wishes had come true.

"I can't live like this!" I moaned. "I've only had one day of bad luck and I'm going crazy."

Vanessa snorted and adjusted her scarf. "You don't have bad luck! That fortune-teller has no idea what she's talking about. She said I'd have a hundred eyes on me this morning, and was anybody watching me? No."

"Actually . . ." Tim reached for her scarf, which had a peacock-tail print. "In Greek mythology there was a creature named Argus who had a hundred eyes all over his body. When he died, his eyes were put on the peacock tail."

I gasped so hard I felt light-headed. "V, the hundred eyes are on your scarf! And your scarf has been on you all morning! Madame Delphi was right!"

Vanessa scowled at Tim. "Are you happy with yourself?"

"Yes." He smiled. "One of my uncle Theo's stories was actually useful!" At the ceaseless glare from V, he added, "But it doesn't matter. There's no such thing as luck, good or bad."

I turned to Vanessa. "Can I see your folding mirror?"

"Uh . . . sure," she said with a confused look. She handed it over, and I opened it, placing it on the ground at Tim's feet.

"Break the mirror," I told him.

"Hey!" said Vanessa.

"Ooh," said Heather in a soft voice.

Tim snorted. "Seriously?"

"Yeah. Break the mirror. Stomp on it." I leaned back in my seat. "It's seven years' bad luck, but since you don't believe in that . . ." I shrugged.

"Fine. Whatever." Tim snorted again and shifted his foot so it hovered over the mirror. Heather hid her face behind her fingers as Tim licked his lips and took a deep breath. When he let it out, he moved his foot away and picked up the mirror.

"Ha! I knew it!" I said.

"You know nothing." He shot me a withering look. "I just don't think I need to ruin Vanessa's stuff to prove a point," he replied, handing her the mirror.

I gave him a smug smile. "And you don't want seven years of bad luck."

He squinted at me. "How many years have we known each other?"

"Five."

"And I've made it through *that* bad luck okay," he said with a wicked grin.

Heather and Vanessa laughed. I smiled. "All right, I walked into that one. But you don't have bad luck! You got to see Adrenaline Dennis."

"And it was totally awesome!" Tim leaned forward, forgetting his sandwich as he told us all about watching Adrenaline do his trick moves midair.

I listened intently, but Heather smiled with a faraway look in her eyes and V lost all interest within the first minute, using the time to clean out her purse. When Tim reached the last line of his story, she looked back up and said, "Cool! Sounds like fun."

Tim smirked at her. "You didn't hear a word I said."

"I did!" Vanessa argued. "Adrenaline let you ride his practice bike."

"He let me sit on the back while he steered," corrected Tim.

"And he showed you his wrench collection."

"His whole toolbox, actually."

V gave him a withering look. "Seriously? Don't I get a little credit? Heather didn't even stay on the planet for your story."

Heather blushed. "I'm sorry, Tim. I got distracted when you said Adrenaline was working on his take-out move."

"Because you've been working on the same one?" I asked. "You know there's room in the motocross world for both of you."

My friends laughed.

"No, silly." Heather tweaked my arm. "Because it reminds me of something that happened during the holiday parade. Something I didn't tell you guys about on Saturday." She looked at me and V.

On Saturday nights, ever since we were in elementary, Heather, V, and I get together for pizza and movies at Heather's house. We call it Musketeer Movies because the three of us are as close as the Three Musketeers.

At the mention of a potentially juicy tidbit, V and I shifted closer.

"What happened?" I asked.

Heather tucked her hair behind her ear and smiled shyly. "Emmett asked if he could take me out on a for-real date."

We clapped and squealed. Well . . . V and I did. Tim just said, "About time."

Then Vanessa and I hit Heather with a volley of questions.

"When did it happen?"

"What did he say?"

"What did you say?"

"What were you wearing?"

"Does anyone need their purse cleaned out?" asked Tim with a yawn.

I elbowed him. "Be nice! This is a good thing."

"I know." He nodded. "But I also know this conversation will take an emotional turn, complete with random crying and laughing and the statement 'You guys would make such a cute couple!'" He got to his feet and picked up his tray. "So I'll leave you to it and finish my lunch in the newsroom." Tim paused and smiled at Heather. "Although, you two would make a cute couple."

She smiled at him before turning to me and V. "Emmett asked when we were first getting on the parade float, so . . . I was wearing my choir robes to answer your question."

"I've seen those choir robes," said V, wrinkling her nose. "If he still asked you out, he must really like you."

Heather and I laughed, and she continued her story.

"Emmett said he was going to be too nervous to perform if he didn't ask right then."

"Awww!" said V and I together.

"So he pulled me aside—"

"Awww!"

It was probably best that Tim had left.

"And asked me to go out this Friday!"

V and I watched her expectantly.

"Did you say yes?" Vanessa finally asked.

Heather paused for dramatic effect and then nodded with a huge grin.

"Yay!" I said, leaning over and hugging her.

"Let me know if you need any help getting ready," said V, hugging her too. "I'm so happy for you!"

"And like Tim says, it's about time," I added.

Heather nodded. "I decided that this year I'm going to try to be more adventurous . . . one of the reasons I agreed to go with you guys to see Madame Delphi."

I didn't bother pointing out that we'd had to practically drag her kicking and screaming.

"I like that," said V, smiling. "In fact, I'll try to be better this year too. I'm going to really put some effort into KV Fashions."

"That should make Katie happy," I said. "And I'm going to not have any more bad luck for the rest of the year!"

"Good for you!" cheered Heather.

Within ten minutes, I failed my resolution.

As soon as the lunch bell rang and we stood up, I accidentally put my hand on the front of my tray and flipped it toward me. I tried to back away, but ketchup still splattered my shirt, and when I stepped aside I knocked over my chair. I tripped and would've impaled myself on one of the legs if V hadn't grabbed my arm.

"You are not having your best day," she said, as if I didn't know.

"Maybe instead of declaring no bad luck for the year you should start small," said Heather. "Like no bad luck for the next sixty seconds."

I nodded and wiped my shirt with a napkin, smearing mustard over the ketchup stain.

"Five seconds is a solid goal too," said V.

I sighed and dropped the napkin on the table.

"Don't worry," she said. "I have a stain-removing pen. For now, let's just get you out of here. I can't watch your clothes suffer anymore, and this place is Stain Central."

The three of us hurried down the hall, my friends on either side of me like Secret Service on a detail.

"Hey, I know what'll cheer you up," said Heather, squeezing my arm. "The first advice requests of the year!" She pointed to the drop box where students left their questions, but when we looked inside, it was empty.

"I can't catch a break!" I said.

"That's because Tim has the requests," said Heather, glancing past us into the classroom. She frowned. "Along with a hat I hoped we'd never see again."

"A hat?" asked V as she and I both turned to look at Tim.

He was sorting slips of paper and wearing a plastic construction hat. It was the same kind of hat Mary Patrick had worn when she wanted us to toughen up to criticism at the start of the school year.

"Oh no," I said.

"Oh yes," said Mary Patrick, stepping into the doorway with three more hats. "We have a newspaper contest to win."

CHAPTER 3

Brooke Versus

" Contests, actually," Mary Patrick corrected herself. "I expect to crush the other schools in *both* categories." She smashed her fist into her palm.

"Calm down, Godzilla," said Tim without looking up from the advice requests.

"I thought the hard hats were for Toughen Up Tuesday," I said.

When my friends and I had started at the paper, we'd gone through a rite of passage, facing and dealing with criticism after the first issue was printed. The hard hat had been filled with all kinds of feedback from students.

"It started out that way," Mary Patrick confessed. "But my mom said I had to use them more than once, and it was either this or form a small construction crew."

Heather, V, and I looked at one another. Then we put on the hats.

"So what are these contests?" asked Heather as we took our seats. "Are we up against different schools in the area?"

"In the state!" corrected Mary Patrick, spreading her arms wide. "And after that, the Midwest! And after that, the country!"

Tim leaned toward me. "I can't tell . . . is she being crazy or optimistic?"

Mary Patrick narrowed her eyes. "I think you'll change your attitude when you hear what the prize is." She flounced off to the front of the classroom as the warning bell rang and people hurried to their seats.

Mrs. H clapped her hands to get our attention while Mary Patrick gave stern looks to those who took more than a millisecond to get quiet.

"Good afternoon, staffers, and welcome back to Lincoln Middle School's favorite newspaper! We are going to have an excellent spring term, and it starts with a newspaper contest and a chance to win . . ." She paused and said in a whisper, "Five thousand dollars."

Instantly, the entire class was abuzz, including my team.

"Did she say five thousand dollars?" asked Tim.

"Each?" asked Vanessa with wide eyes. "As in . . . I could buy both a left *and* a right Louboutin?"

I grinned. "Even if it's by team and we split the money four ways, that's, like, a thousand—"

"Twelve hundred and fifty," said Heather.

"—a person!" I finished. "That's still a lot of

money!" I glanced up at Mrs. H, eager to hear more.

She and Mary Patrick were smiling at the response from the class.

"Looks like we might have a little interest in the contest," said Mrs. H. "There will actually be two ways to compete. We'll be competing for Best Overall Newspaper, and you may also compete for Best Section or Best Photo." She looked at Stefan Marshall and Gil when she said this.

As Mrs. H kept talking, Mary Patrick handed a stack of papers to the first person in each row to pass back. Mrs. H raised her voice to be heard above the shuffling of paper and the whispers of conversation.

"Mary Patrick and I think our first issue for the new year could be an excellent chance to take Best Overall Newspaper, and for the section contest, each team is free to use either their piece from that paper or past segments."

Tim raised his hand. "Who gets the five thousand dollars?"

"For the overall contest, the money will go to the school," said Mrs. H. "But for the section contests and photo contest, a smaller award of one thousand dollars will be divided among the team members."

More chaos erupted from the class.

"A thousand dollars all for me!" said Stefan Marshall, rubbing his hands together. He was in charge of sports, photography, and patting himself on the back.

And he seemed to have forgotten he didn't work on his sections alone.

Instantly Tim and Gil spoke up.

"Hey, backup photographer here!" said Gil, pointing to himself.

"And backup sports writer!" said Tim, waving a hand. "There's no way you get all that money. Unless you kill us first." He chuckled but then grew serious, holding his pen like a weapon.

"That's not fair!" spoke up Felix, the front-page team leader. "Stefan writes for sports and does photography. He gets two chances to win."

"Yeah, and Gil does photography and lifestyle with the horoscopes," someone else pointed out.

"And Tim—"

Mrs. H held up a hand. "Each student will only be allowed to compete for one category. So Stefan, Gil, Tim . . . you'll have to choose."

"Fine," said Stefan. "I'm going with sports. Nothing can beat my interview with Adrenaline Dennis."

Mrs. H looked at Tim, who instantly said, "Lifestyle."

"Darn right!" I held up my hand, and Tim high-fived it.

"Gil?" Mary Patrick asked him. "Will you be with the lifestyle girls?"

"And guy!" chimed in Tim.

"Or will you represent photography?" she continued, ignoring him.

Gil shrugged at me and my friends. "Sorry, guys, but I think I'll have a stronger chance with photography."

I couldn't blame him. A couple months back, Gil had submitted a photo for a city exhibit and someone had bought his piece before the show even opened.

"It's okay," V told him with a reassuring smile. The rest of our team nodded.

"Now that we've settled that," said Mrs. H, "I'd really like you all to think hard about how you can make this issue the best that's ever been read."

"Remember, we're real journalists," added Mary Patrick. "We need stories of scandal and intrigue."

"Maybe not scandal," said Mrs. H with a frown.

"Intrigue, then," amended Mary Patrick. "Most of our competitors will be writing about New Year's resolutions and back-to-school reminders. We need to bring the heat!"

Mrs. H nodded. "Please break into your small groups and discuss what you'll contribute. I'll be coming around to talk with each of you."

There was a dragging of chairs as everyone joined their teams.

"Two-fifty apiece," said Tim, moving his desk closer. "Wow!"

"*If* we're the best section," I reminded him. "So do we want to go with something new or turn in one of our old issues?" I glanced around at my team.

"Can we do both?" asked Heather. "Have an old issue in mind, and if we think it's better than the new issue, we can turn it in for the section contest?"

"I like it!" I said. "Which of our old issues?"

She thought for a moment. "I like the one we did for Thanksgiving."

"That one was pretty good," said Vanessa. She held up her finger. "But, I think you mean the one from right around Halloween."

"I'm gonna go with the one before winter break," said Tim.

I frowned. "And I think our first full issue was the best."

My friends and I watched one another, waiting for someone to concede.

"Let's take a vote," V finally said.

I nodded and opened my notebook. "But you can't vote for the one you just suggested."

We all worked in silence for a moment, and then I collected the choices my friends had written down.

"Okay, Vanessa liked—"

"Hey! This should be anonymous!" said V. Then she corrected herself. "I mean . . . how do you know that's even me?"

I turned the paper so she could see. "Because whoever mysteriously suggested this wrote in sparkly, purple pen."

V covered the sparkly, purple pen she was holding with a folder. "It was Tim's."

He raised an eyebrow. "I just got over the major drama of telling people I'm a tights-wearing folk dancer. Do I really need to be the guy who writes with sparkly, purple pen too?"

I cleared my throat. "Anyway, V suggested the issue where she gave advice on fitting in when you have braces." I lowered the page. "Which was the Halloween one. Which I told you that you couldn't suggest."

She grinned sheepishly. "I was hoping you hadn't remembered."

I looked at Tim and Heather. "Did you guys submit suggestions about pieces you wrote too?"

They were both quiet for a moment, and then

Heather slowly reached across the table and dragged her piece of paper back.

Tim pressed his lips together. "You can just throw mine away. I accidentally sneezed in it."

"Guys," I said with a sigh. "You can't just suggest the issues where you looked good."

"What did you suggest?" asked Vanessa, reaching for my paper.

"That's not important." I crumpled it in one hand and stood up. "I'm going to grab our back issues so we can review them and see which are best for the team."

I walked to the bookshelves where we kept boxes of old newspapers and removed one with the previous year written on it. It felt like we'd been churning out issues forever, but I was surprised to find only a dozen for the previous semester. When I got back to the table, my friends and I pored over them.

"I think we can agree to leave out the one

where Heather and V had people filling in for them," I said.

"Thank you," said Heather with a smile.

"One down, eleven to go," said Tim. "What about the first issue for the short week?"

"The one with Sir Stinks a Lot?" I asked.

My friends laughed.

"That would be it," he said with a grin.

I shook my head. "We can't, because some of the advice I gave wasn't accurate, remember? Abel pointed it out to me, and I almost murdered him?"

"And then you guys started dating!" said Heather with a dreamy expression. "So romantic."

"How about this one?" asked V, holding up an issue. "Brooke gave a great answer about eating healthy, Heather crushed it with her advice on dealing with a new stepparent, and Tim's answer about how to grow a mustache was hilarious."

I smiled and read over V's shoulder in my best

announcer voice. "'You want a mustache, friend? I've got the perfect solution: Tim's Wait-Awhile Whisker Water! Just put a drop on your upper lip, wait awhile, and hair magically begins to grow! All for the low, low price of twenty-nine ninety-five.'" In a softer voice, I added. "'Results may take up to three years.'"

My friends laughed, and Tim shook his head. "I never made a single sale."

I took the paper from V and read the responses to the other letters. She was right; they were all great. "What do you guys think?" I asked, passing the paper around.

Heather and Tim both glanced at it and nodded.

"Awesome!" I took the paper back and folded it in half. "We'll use these if we don't like the pieces we contribute for our best issue ever."

Tim clucked his tongue. "You can't say it like that. You have to mean it!" He cupped his hands around his mouth and fake shouted, "The best issue ever . . . ever . . . ever." He echoed his words, growing quieter after each one.

We laughed.

The sound of happy people must've been too much for Mary Patrick because she stormed over.

"What's with all the merrymaking? You haven't won the contest yet. All your heads should be down!"

"In prayer to the newspaper gods?" I asked.

"In concentration!" she said with a frown.

"For your information, we've already picked the piece we want to enter *if* we decide not to go with what we run in this week's issue," I said.

Mary Patrick crossed her arms. "And what are you running in this week's issue?"

Normally I would've had a snappy comeback, but she looked positively murderous.

I smiled up at her while reaching for Tim's

and Heather's heads, bowing them toward their desks. I raised an eyebrow at Vanessa, and we bowed our heads too.

"That's what I thought," said Mary Patrick, snorting air out of her nostrils. "For us to win, every team has to give their all. Save your laughter for later."

She spun on her heel and walked off.

"Geez, what's her problem?" asked Tim, lifting his head while he wrote on a sheet of paper. "You'd think we worked for the *Chicago Tribune*."

"Mary Patrick graduates at the end of the semester," Heather reminded him. "And she'll be starting over at the bottom in high school. She's probably just scared."

"The people in high school should be scared," he said.

V looked at what Tim was writing. "What's 'pickle cactus membrane'?"

"It's what I write whenever I'm pretending to

work," he said with a smile.

"Well, how about we actually work?" I asked, reaching into the advice pile. "We need to find questions that require more than a one-word answer."

"So, *not* 'Should I get a tattoo?'" asked Heather with a smile, putting the question aside.

"What about this one for me?" asked Vanessa. "'Dear Lincoln's Letters, I want to change my look for the new year. Where do I start?'"

I rubbed my chin. "I don't know. It doesn't feel . . . deep enough."

Tim snorted. "You want to go deep when you're talking about someone's appearance?"

"True." I pointed at him. "But I'm sure there are better questions out there so V can talk about being happy with who you are outside *and* in."

She looked up. "You mean like the issue where I helped the girl with the braces?"

"We're not running that piece," I said.

"How come?" She threw her hands in the air. "I was good!"

"Tim was not!" I responded.

"Hey!" he said. "All my advice is top-notch."

I found the newspaper issue in question and read aloud his response. "'Dear Snot Rocket, go for distance, not speed. Confidentially yours, Tim Antonides.'" I lowered the paper and stared at him.

"Top-notch and sometimes disgusting," he amended.

"Keep looking." I pointed to the advice requests. "And if you pick any with the words *booger* or *fart*, I'll sic Mary Patrick on you."

We all sat quietly, pondering advice requests, and before we knew it, the bell to end class rang.

Heather groaned. "I didn't find anything that stood out."

"There's always tomorrow," I reminded her.

"Plus the ones people sent through the website."

On top of being a print publication, the *Lincoln Log* is also online, where the advice column isn't limited to half a page, so we can help even more kids.

"How did you do?" I asked V.

"I found two that might work." She showed them to me, and I nodded.

"Go with the one about why her friend looks better in different shades of makeup," I said. "You can say we're all unique from the inside out."

Vanessa laughed. "I was thinking the same thing!"

"How unique," commented Tim.

I stuck my tongue out at him. "Did *you* come up with anything?"

"Not yet," he admitted. "So far everyone's wondering about Valentine's Day."

"That's still a month away!" I marveled.

He shrugged. "As soon as Christmas ended,

my parents started stocking Valentine's junk in their grocery stores. Everyone's just ready for the next holiday."

"Not me," said Vanessa. "I spent way too much at Christmas. My purse has nothing in it now but some makeup and a Band-Aid."

"I think you need to be carrying something bigger than a Band-Aid," I teased. "Maybe a tiny ambulance?"

"You should talk, Bad Luck Brooke," Tim said with a smirk.

V smacked him in the chest.

"Ow! What was that for?"

"Why'd you have to bring that up?" she asked. "Brooke probably forgot all about it."

She was right. I *had* forgotten, but it wasn't as if Tim bringing it up made me unlucky again. Even if he hadn't said anything, I still would've banged my elbow on the door frame a minute later.

"Are you okay?" Heather asked, making a pained face on my behalf.

"I will be when I can get out of this building and onto the soccer field," I said as we walked to history together.

No matter how bad a day I'm having, being able to run and kick and get my adrenaline flowing always makes me feel better. Mom calls it endorphins. I call it soccer!

I managed to survive the rest of the school day, and when I climbed into Mom's car, I breathed a sigh of relief.

"Safe at last," I said.

She smiled. "I'll take that as a compliment."

"You would not believe the day I had," I said, leaning against the seat.

I told her while we drove to the soccer complex, pointing out every bruise and stain that had happened as I went.

"Oh, honey, I'm sorry," said Mom. "Sounds like you had a bad day."

"A bad *luck* day," I pointed out.

Mom gave me a look. "Brooke, we talked about this."

"Yeah, but if you'd taken a highlighter to the face you might change your mind," I said. "One or two things going wrong I can understand. But a flood of them?" I shook my head. "The universe has got it in for me, Mom."

She pulled the car into the parking lot. "I don't think so, but if that's what you want to believe . . . good luck at practice!" Mom leaned over and kissed the top of my head.

In the winter, it's too cold and snowy to play outdoors, so we practice at an indoor field with three pitches separated by glass walls. It's not entirely realistic, since if you kick a ball out of bounds outdoors, it won't come back and hit you in the face. But if you want to take state like we do, you have to play whenever and wherever you can.

In just a few minutes I managed to get changed, use the restroom, put my hair up, *and* put on my cleats while the other girls were standing around only halfway in uniform. Some were wearing jeans and soccer jerseys; others were wearing shorts and sweaters. All of them were busy talking. Since I'm captain, it's up to me to make sure everyone's dressed and ready for warm-ups right on time. I was just about to say something when I felt a hard tap on my shoulder. "Hey, *Captain*."

Ugh. Lacey Black: the thorn in my side. No, not thorn. The entire rosebush in my side.

I turned to face her, and she let out a massive sneeze.

Right. In. My face.

"Gross!" I scrubbed my cheeks against my sleeve and scowled at her. "You got my attention just so you could do that?"

Lacey sniffled. "Actually, no, I was going to say something, but that was an added bonus." She frowned. "And the least you could do is offer me a tissue!"

"What do you want, Lacey?"

"What happened to your hand?" she smirked. "Playing soccer upside d—ACHOO!" She sneezed again, but this time I was prepared and held up a towel.

I peeked around one side. "Your insults aren't as effective with snot running out of your nose."

"I know, darn it!" Lacey sniffled again. "I must be allergic to you." Her expression took on its usual sass. "But my point was that you play soccer upside down because you're really bad at it."

"Okay, now you're gross *and* wrong," I said, tossing the towel at her. "Everyone on this team earned their spot. Including me."

"Just like you earned your captaincy?" She crossed her arms. "Must be nice to be coach's pet." She said the last part loud enough for everyone to hear.

The old Brooke would've challenged Lacey to a contest to prove who was better, but now that I was captain, I had to act like it. And that meant rising above silly squabbles.

I climbed on a bench and cupped my hands around my mouth. "Come on, Strikers! Let's get going!"

A couple of my teammates started moving around, but then they stopped and started chatting again.

"Guys!" I clapped my hands. "There are free puppies outside!"

"Really?" someone asked, heading for the exit in her school clothes.

"No!" I stopped her. "Go back and change. All

of you!" I walked from girl to girl, picking up jerseys and socks and forcing them into the hands of their owners.

A captain is supposed to inspire her team and get them working together.

I inspired them to give me dirty looks and grumble about me together.

Close enough.

When everyone finally made it out of the locker room, Coach didn't look pleased.

But as it turned out, his upset had nothing to do with us.

"Ladies," he said. "I have some bad news. Kayla broke her leg skiing with her parents last week."

The cluster of girls around Coach buzzed with worried conversation.

"Is she okay?" I asked.

Coach nodded. "She will be, but she'll also be out for the rest of the season."

That wasn't good. Kayla was one of our star players. She was a striker like Lacey and me, which meant we'd have to move someone up in the ranks to fill her position. Apparently, Coach already had someone in mind.

"Brin, I want you to move from midfield to forward," he said to a stocky blond girl.

She nodded, but Lacey scoffed and sneezed. "You can't make a middie a forward, Coach! They're not fast enough. Besides, who's going to take *her* place?"

Coach pointed to one of the girls from our second string. "Jenny, are you up for the challenge of starting midfielder?"

Jenny stepped forward. "Yes, sir!"

"Oh, this is gonna be great," mumbled Lacey in a voice so low only the people beside her could hear.

"We've still got time to train them up," I said. "Relax."

"Ladies, I hope you enjoyed your holidays," continued Coach. "But now it's time to get serious. We've got a championship to win, right?"

"Right!" we all yelled.

"We've got to work hard to get it, right?"

"Right!"

Coach blew his whistle and pointed to the field. "Warm-up drills. Do 'em like Brooke calls 'em!"

I trotted backward onto the turf. "Okay, everyone, I—ahhh!"

One second I was on my feet, the next I was falling on my butt.

Brooke Jacobs, the one-girl tumbling act.

I wish I could've blamed it on a gopher hole or some bad landscaping, but we were inside. On fake grass.

"How did that happen?" I asked as one of the girls ran forward to give me a hand up.

"Looks like you stepped in something oily,"

the girl said, examining my cleat. "That's too bad."

Too bad. Bad luck. Could it have followed me to my safe place?

Someone else threw me a towel, and I wiped the bottoms of both my cleats.

"Brooke, are you okay?" asked Coach.

I got to my feet and smiled at everyone. "Absolutely," I said. "Let's start with a juggling drill. Everyone grab a practice ball."

In soccer we don't juggle with our hands; we use our feet, ankles, and knees to keep the ball in the air.

Everyone grabbed one ball while I stood in the background and waited my turn.

"Here, clumsy." Lacey shoved a ball into my chest.

I frowned at her and muttered, "Thanks," while I positioned myself at the front of the group. "Ready?" I called to the girls, holding the ball above my knee. "Let's go for thirty seconds!" I pointed to the clock on the wall. "Begin!"

I dropped the ball and lifted my knee to bounce it, but I must have used more force than I thought, because I launched the ball up and over my shoulder. I chased after it and tried again, dropping the ball on my foot this time. Instead of hitting the inside curve of my ankle and going vertical, it went horizontal and nailed some girl in the back of the leg.

"Sorry, my bad!" I said when she yelped.

I took my time fetching the ball and watched the clock, waiting for the thirty seconds to end. When it did, I scooped up the ball and said, "Okay, let's switch to a passing drill, two lines side by side. Left line has the ball, switching at the center line."

I formed the start of the left line, and Lacey formed the start of the right.

This time it was Brin who messed up. As

much as I hated to admit it, Lacey was right; Brin wasn't as fast as she needed to be. She did a pretty good job keeping up, but by the time she and her partner reached the center line, Brin was at least a good yard behind.

After a couple more drills, it was time to run some practice plays. Luckily Jenny already knew them, and Brin just had to get used to a different position.

"You're doing great!" I shouted to her as we trotted down the field. I kicked the ball from one foot to the other and arced it toward her.

Brin scrambled to catch up to it, but the ball was too quick, and the other team got possession.

"Come on, Brin!" screeched Lacey. "Get the ball!"

Brin tucked her head low and raced after it as a girl from the other team approached Jenny, the replacement midfielder.

"They're going for the weak links!" Lacey shouted to me.

I nodded and called to Jenny, "Don't watch her shoulders, watch her feet! That's where the ball's going!"

Sure enough, the girl with the ball faked left and ran right, but Jenny did the opposite of what I told her, and the girl charged past.

"Come on!" Lacey threw her hands in the air and then had a sneezing fit.

"She'll get the hang of it," I said.

Coach blew his whistle, and we all ran off the field.

"Good hustle out there," he said. "But let's watch our passing." He looked at me. "And listen to our captain." He smiled at Jenny and lifted the whistle to his lips. "Let's run it again!"

We headed back out onto the field, and this time Lacey got possession of the ball. Brin and I ran down the field on opposite sides of her, waiting for a pass play. She kicked it to me, and I dodged a striker from the other team, making for an unprotected spot in the center of the field. At the same time, Lacey surged forward so I could pass the ball to her.

I glanced around for Brin and pointed to where I wanted her to be. She pointed right back at me. I gave her a confused look.

And then I collided with something solid and sneezy.

Lacey was crouched in a sneezing fit, and I flipped over her with a shout of surprise. My hands went out to break my fall, and the one that hit the ground first, my right one, twisted a little to the side when I landed. Pain shot up my arm as I crumpled to the ground.

Coach immediately blew the whistle, and all movement shifted from running toward the goal to running toward me.

"Is she okay?"

"Is she dead?"

"I didn't do it on purpose! I swear!"

That was Lacey, shaking her head over and over.

"I'm fine," I muttered, rolling onto my back to look up at everyone. "I just hurt my wrist a little." I tried to put weight on it and winced. "Maybe a lot."

Coach crouched beside me. "How's your head? Any pain anywhere else?" He felt my skull from different angles. Then he held one of my eyes open wide and studied it.

"One of her knees is bleeding," someone commented.

"That's nothing," I said. "My knees are half scab anyway."

Coach had me bend my legs and rotate my ankles before he felt confident helping me to my feet. Then he had me bend my arms and rotate my shoulders.

"Everything else is fine," I assured him. "It's just my wrist."

I held it out and could already see it starting to swell.

Coach gingerly touched the skin. "Feels a little warm. Let's get some ice on it and call your parents, okay? I want them to take you to a doctor to make sure it's not broken."

We turned to go, and Lacey appeared by my side.

"That wasn't my fault. *You* tripped over me."

"Lacey, not now," said Coach with a flicker of annoyance.

"Okay, but I didn't do that," she said, pointing at my wrist.

"No, you didn't," I agreed. "It was bad luck."

"I'll say," said Coach.

But he had no idea.

CHAPTER

4

Beware of Brooke

At least my bad luck had a limit. My wrist turned out to be sprained, and I'd have to wear a splint for a few weeks, but that was the worst of it.

"Can I still play soccer?" I asked the doctor.

"I wouldn't," she said. "Jostling your arm so much will be pretty painful."

Okay, I was wrong. *That* was the worst of it.

"I can play through the pain," I reassured her. Then I looked up at Dad, who'd picked me up on his way home. "You know me."

He nodded. "Yes. I know you're stubborn."

He spoke to the doctor. "Do you have anything to treat *that*?"

"Very funny," I said, holding out my arm so the doctor could fit my wrist with the splint.

"If there was a treatment for stubbornness, I'd be out of business," she said with a smile. "It causes a lot of injuries." I started to pull my arm back, but she placed a hand on it. "One sec. Let's get your sling on."

"What?" I watched her open a drawer and pull out a piece of blue canvas with a white strap. "I have to wear a splint *and* a sling?"

"The sling is only for a couple of days," said the doctor as she eased my splinted arm into it.

"But if Coach sees my arm in a sling, he definitely won't let me play!" I glanced up at Dad.

He got nose to nose with me. "You aren't listening. You can't play right now, sweetheart."

I slumped over, and Dad put his arms around me. "But you can still watch," he added.

"It's not the same." I slid down from the examination table, and Dad draped my coat over my shoulders.

"Hang in there, Brooke," said the doctor, patting me on my good arm. "Soccer will still be around in a few weeks."

I gave a halfhearted smile, which is sometimes all grown-ups really want, and trudged out of the exam room.

My soccer team had already lost one striker, and now I was out for a few weeks. And we had a game coming up before I'd be better! It was going to be up to Lacey, Brin, and whoever Coach found to replace me. And honestly, I didn't know if a completely different starting line would be good enough.

When we got home, Mom hugged me and fussed over my injury, which earned me sympathy pizza for dinner and an ice-cream sundae for dessert.

"By the way, Abel called the house," she said when I was polishing off the last bite of ice cream. "He said you didn't answer your phone after practice, so he got worried, and when I told him what happened, he got *really* worried."

"What?" I pushed my chair back. "He called and you're just telling me now?"

I hurried down the hall to get my book bag.

I'm not gonna lie. My wrist felt like someone was stabbing it with a thousand needles.

"Ugh. Stupid doctor, being right!" I muttered as I fished through my bag with my good hand.

I found my phone and saw that it had somehow been switched to silent mode. A string of texts, missed calls, and voice mails was waiting for me. I had voice mails from Vanessa, a couple from Abel, and one from . . . Mary Patrick.

"Oh no." I listened to the message she'd left, wondering what could've possibly gone wrong.

"Brooke," said Mary Patrick by way of greeting. "The team leads and I are meeting before school tomorrow to talk about the contest issue. You need to be there."

"Everything okay?" Mom stepped into the hall.

I nodded and kept listening. "Mary Patrick wants to meet before school." I groaned and deleted the voice mail. "Half an hour before!"

Mom clucked her tongue. "Looks like someone's going to sleep early."

"Fine with me," I said. "The sooner this day ends, the better."

After I'd gotten ready for bed, I called Abel back.

"I'm sorry I missed your messages!" I said. "My phone was on silent, and then I was at the hospital."

"I heard!" he said. "Are you okay?"

"No. My wrist is messed up, and I can't play soccer for a few weeks!" I lamented. "Even after I begged my dad."

"Aw, that stinks," said Abel. "But do you really think you'd play well right now?"

"One time I played with a head cold and still scored two goals," I informed him.

"Probably because you were sick and nobody wanted to touch the cootie ball."

I snickered. "Quit trying to make me feel better!"

"I'm so sorry," he said in a mock humble tone. "I will never comfort you again."

I smiled. "So tell me something good that happened to you today. I'll steal your happiness and make it my own!" I gave an evil cackle, and this time Abel laughed.

"Well, I started cranking up the treadmill so I can run a little faster," he said.

Abel is one of our track stars, and this spring

he wants to beat a bunch of distance records.

"That's great! What else?"

"The clubs section of the paper is suddenly really interested in Young Sherlocks."

"They are?" I asked. Then I narrowed my eyes. "Wait. They just want to use Young Sherlocks to win the section contest of the newspaper competition. Don't give them what they want!"

"But it's good exposure for the club," argued Abel. "We haven't solved a case since Thanksgiving."

I decided to put it another way. "Look, if you help them, you're going against me. Don't you want me to win?"

Abel sighed into the phone. "Fine, but it's going to cost you fifty hugs."

I laughed. "That's pretty expensive, but I think I can manage."

Abel told me about the rest of his day until my parents came by to say good night.

"I'll see you tomorrow," I told Abel, ending the call. Then I smiled up at Mom and Dad.

"You're looking cheerier," said Dad.

"I was talking to Abel."

"Oooh." Dad batted his eyelashes and made a kissy face. I rolled my eyes.

"I'm guessing the bad luck is over now that little cartoon hearts are in the air?" asked Mom.

Even though she was joking, I smiled. "It might just be."

Ten hours later I was back in the kitchen for breakfast, grabbing a glass of juice to go with my plate of eggs. I whistled while I poured, having gotten out of bed and dressed without falling or getting my head stuck in a sock.

"Look at you, wide-awake and with your clothes on the right direction!" said Dad.

"Yep!" Since I only had one good hand, I balanced my glass of juice on the empty part of my plate and carried it to a counter where Dad had propped open a box of doughnuts. "I think things are turning around."

I bent over the box of doughnuts and grabbed a powdered one with my teeth.

"Hey!" Mom poked me in the side. "We're not bobbing for doughnuts here. Use your fingers."

I tried to answer her with the doughnut between my teeth, but I inhaled powdered sugar and started coughing. The doughnut fell out of my mouth and I tried to catch it, shifting so that the juice glass tipped off the plate and fell onto the floor. It shattered when it hit the tile, sending shards of glass and splashes of juice everywhere.

Mom patted me on the back while Dad picked up the bigger broken pieces.

"Deep breaths," she said.

I did what she said, coughing as I squatted to pick up the doughnut, which now featured glass sprinkles and an orange glaze. Unfortunately,

Mom knew me all too well.

"Don't you dare eat that," she warned.

"I wasn't going to," I lied, throwing the doughnut in the trash.

Dad put a fresh one on my plate. "Not to rush you, but I've got to leave for work in ten minutes, so if you want to ride with me you'd better hustle."

"Don't eat too fast," said Mom as I wolfed down my food. "And brush your teeth."

I settled for rinsing with a fresh glass of orange juice.

Mom sighed as I put my dishes in the sink. "Good enough, I guess."

I kissed her cheek, grabbed my bag, and went to throw on my coat but paused when I remembered I was wearing a stupid sling. "Um . . . Mom?" I flapped my injured arm at her, like a bird with a bad wing.

Mom chuckled and wrapped my coat around me, buttoning it. "It's like you're five years old again and I'm dressing you for kindergarten."

I curled my lip, and Dad leaned over Mom's shoulder. "Pretty sure you're not making this easier," he told her.

"Oh. Right," said Mom, stepping back. "Have a good day at school, my incredibly grown-up daughter."

I cracked a smile. "Thanks, Mom." I nodded to Dad. "Let's go."

He followed me out the door and was quick enough to pull me back when a sheet of snow came sliding off the roof.

"Wow. You really are on a bad streak," he said, glancing up.

"That's what I've been trying to tell you!"

Dad saw the frustrated look on my face and kissed the top of my head. "Sorry, honey, that was just an expression. This will pass."

"When?" I asked. "I've got soccer, newspaper, and school to worry about."

Dad pointed me toward the car. "I don't know, but until then, you've got to keep your head up." He lifted my chin and winked. "So you can watch for falling snow."

"But then I won't see any holes in the ground," I pointed out. "I could trip and fall."

"And Mom and I will pick you up."

"That might turn out to be a full-time job," I informed him.

"Then we'll take shifts." He held the car door open for me.

My morning mayhem had put me behind schedule again, so I broke into a run as soon as I got to school. But it was so painful to jostle my wrist up and down that I had to stop and settle for a fast walk. I slowed my pace just outside the newsroom, took a few deep breaths, and smoothed my hair back before strolling in casually.

Mary Patrick was sitting at a desk surrounded by the other team leaders. When she saw me, she scowled. "You're—"

"One minute late?" I finished, glancing at the clock.

"Let's just start our strategy meeting," she said, getting up and walking to the front whiteboard. "I've competed in this contest for the last two years, and both times we came close but didn't win. I think it's because we lack something special." She picked up a marker and uncapped it. "We need to find out what it is."

She wrote: *originality and innovation*.

Then she turned to face the rest of us. "I need ideas, people. Our paper needs great content, but it also needs to stand out from the crowd. Make it happen."

She put the cap back on her marker, and

everyone picked up their book bags. I didn't move a muscle but watched in confusion as people headed for the door.

"Wait," I said. "Where's everyone going?" I grabbed Stefan's arm as he passed me. "What's happening?"

"Meeting's over," he said, giving me a strange look. "Unless you want to stay and listen to Mary Patrick rant about how the *Galena Gazette* stole our victory last year."

"I heard that," said Mary Patrick from where she was sitting at Mrs. H's desk.

Stefan rolled his eyes and walked away. I went in the other direction, straight for Mary Patrick.

"What about the strategy meeting?" I asked.

She looked up from the copy of the *New York Times* she was reading. "That was the strategy meeting. Our strategy is: win."

I stared at her. "You could've just texted that message to me."

"I could have," she agreed. "But then I wouldn't have been guaranteed your attention. You probably would've skimmed my message and kept playing soccer with your cats."

"I would not!" I said. "But . . . that sounds cute, so I probably will now!"

Mary Patrick returned to her reading. "Glad to hear it."

I put my hand in the center of her paper. "Hey, I got up extra early and choked on a doughnut to be here. And I'm injured!" I pointed at my bad arm.

"Did that happen working on your column?" she asked.

"No, it happened at soccer."

She nodded slowly. "I'm quickly losing interest in your point. *Do* you have a new way we can present the *Lincoln Log*?"

I scrunched my face up for a moment and thought.

"Oh this is going to be brilliant. I can already tell," she said, picking her paper back up.

"How about we use a crazy font?" I asked. "Maybe something scary."

"That *idea* is scary," she said. "We're not changing the font to Die Zombie Die or whatever you're considering. We want the paper to look professional."

"How about a full-color issue?" I asked.

Mary Patrick didn't hesitate. "That's great for photos, but does nothing for text." She held up a finger. "And if you even think about suggesting a rainbow font . . ."

"I wasn't going to," I said. "But maybe glitter . . ."

She pointed toward the door. "Out with your terrible ideas. I want brainstorming. This is brainfarting."

Mary Patrick was right. My ideas were terrible. Normally I was great at thinking on the spot.

All I could do was trudge away, backpack still on my shoulder from when I'd walked in two minutes before.

"Unbelievable!" I shouted to nobody in particular. "Brooke's bad luck strikes—" I paused in front of one of the library windows. Heather was sitting inside, nestled in a beanbag chair with a book opened in front of her: *Your Future Foretold*.

"No way," I said, pulling open the library door. "Heather?"

She jumped when she saw me and tried to hide the book behind her until she realized I was wearing a sling.

"What happened?" She scrambled to her feet and hovered her hands around my injured wrist, never actually touching it. "Did the scratch Chelsea gave you get infected?"

"Nope. On top of that, I have a sprained wrist. I crashed into Lacey during soccer and landed on my hand wrong."

"Ouch!" Heather winced. "Are you sure you and Vanessa didn't switch bodies?"

"Is that what your . . . future foretold?" I asked with a smile.

She blushed and pulled the book out. "You can*not* tell Vanessa. She'd never let me hear the end of it."

"Your secret is safe." I took the book from her. "Why are you reading this? I thought the fortune-telling stuff freaked you out."

"It does," she admitted, settling back on the beanbag chair. "But I also liked what Madame Delphi said, and honestly I'm a little mad at myself for not getting a full prediction like you guys."

"Trust me, sometimes you're better off not knowing," I said, flipping through the book. "Are you trying to teach yourself to read tarot cards?"

Heather didn't say anything, and when I looked at her, she was blushing even redder. "I'm

going back to Madame Delphi this afternoon.
I just wanted to read up a bit so I could understand better."

I squished in beside her on the chair. "Really?
You want to know that bad?"

"I have that date with Emmett this weekend,"
she reminded me, hugging her knees to her chest.
"I want to know if it's going to work out."

I frowned. "But . . . isn't part of the fun of dating not knowing what's going to happen?"

Heather smirked. "I already went through
that with Stefan. I think we know how that
turned out." She bumped me. "You should come.
Maybe Madame Delphi could give you some
hope about this bad luck. Or at least tell you how
long it's going to last."

I shook my head. "I have a feeling all she'll
give me is more bad news. And I get enough of
that from Mary Patrick." At the confused look
from Heather I added, "She held a two-minute

meeting today, demanding that the group leaders come up with creative ways to win the newspaper competition."

"Two-minute meeting?" Heather repeated. "She could've just sent a text!"

"That's what I said!" I held up my good hand and Heather high-fived it. "But she wanted our undivided attention."

Heather smiled. "That sounds like her. So what are you doing for the rest of the morning until school starts?"

"Is hiding from life an option?" I pointed toward the librarian's desk. "There's a nice little spot under there where nobody can see me."

"You can't do that," said Heather, poking my leg. "You're Brooke Jacobs, toughest girl alive! Sure you're having some bad luck, but you can handle whatever comes your way!"

But I wasn't handling whatever came my way, so much as barely surviving it. In math class, I was completely lost as the teacher ventured into new territory: algebra.

There was a lot of interest in x and what x was. If x wanted to keep its identity a secret, who were we to try to figure it out? As my math teacher flew through equations, I took notes but might as well have been writing Egyptian hieroglyphs. Nothing made sense, and I glanced around to see who else was confused.

It seemed to be just me.

The rest of the kids in my class had their heads down, solving equations without even looking at the teacher. I stared at the numbers on my page, but my pencil just tapped against the desk and didn't make a move toward the paper.

Then in English, which I'm actually pretty good at, we were reading aloud, and I forgot how to pronounce *venomous*. I'd seen the word a hundred times, I'd said the word a hundred times, but I tripped over it so much I finally changed it to "full of venom." The other kids stared at me like I'd just declared myself Queen Crayon.

Even though my closest friends felt sorry for me, they still laughed when I told them at lunch.

"It's not funny!" I said, but I was smiling.

"I can see Brooke trying to warn someone," said Tim. "Look out! A venonymous snake!"

We all cracked up.

"I wasn't that bad," I said. "And I could say venomous. I just couldn't read it."

"Then remind me to keep you away from the reptile house at the zoo," said V.

I pushed her as everyone laughed again. "My brain was fried from algebra."

"I can help if you want," said Heather. She was in almost all advanced classes.

My eyes lit up. "I would love that."

"And I can teach you to read," said Tim with a grin.

I smiled back. "You wouldn't rather teach me to dance?"

"Ooh!" said V, giving me a high five while Heather giggled behind her hand.

A month ago, a joke like that would've sent Tim into hiding. He was a great dancer but didn't want anyone to know. Now he's proud of it and doesn't mind a little teasing.

"I deserved that one," he admitted with a good-natured grin.

"So enough about me," I said. "V, how's your new fashion plan going?"

In answer, she reached under the table and produced a notebook with patterned fabric swatches fanning out from the sides.

"Glad you asked," she said, "because I wanted your opinion on something. That includes you, Tim."

He eyed the book warily. "Okay, but I can

already tell you penguins with umbrellas do not look good on me." He flicked one of the swatches.

"Oh, no. Those are just place markers," said V. She flipped to the section marked with the penguin print. "Here's what I'm really working on."

Heather, Tim, and I crowded around the notebook. The page showed a sketch of a girl in a tank top with ruffled straps.

"That's cute," Heather said.

"Yeah, I like it," I said.

"Are the straps available without ruffles?" Tim asked.

V smirked. "If they were, then they couldn't do this." She turned the page and pointed to a different image, which showed the ruffles in the straps lengthening into gauzy sleeves.

"Upgrading from cute to super cute!" Heather said.

"This is awesome!" I agreed.

Vanessa showed us a few more ideas she and Katie had been working on until the lunch bell rang and it was time for Journalism. I hung back to say hi to Abel, who had the lunch after mine, while my friends went to check for new advice requests.

"Hey!" he said when he saw me. "Is today a better day?"

"Better now," I said, hugging him. "One hug down, forty-nine to go! How was your morning?"

"I found ten bucks in my jeans!" he said.

"So, it was good, then." I smiled.

"My stomach thought so anyway," he said, rubbing it. "I bought double breakfast." When my eyes widened, he added, "All this training has me starving every morning."

"Yeah, but if you eat too much, won't that just slow you down?" I asked, poking him in the stomach.

Abel frowned and moved my hand. "Don't be mean."

"Aw, I'm sorry. I was just kidding," I said. "But what did you have for breakfast exactly? Because if it's just carbs, you should—"

"Stop telling me what to do. I know how to eat right," he said. "Better than you probably."

I stepped back and crossed my arms. "What's that supposed to mean?"

"Pizza almost every day?" asked Abel.

"I run around enough to make up for it," I said. "*And* I get thin crust."

Abel rolled his eyes. "You're right. That makes all the difference. Thank goodness you give health advice to everyone in school."

My jaw dropped. "Now who's being mean?"

He sighed and rubbed his face with a hand. "Sorry. I'm just . . . can we talk later? I'm starving, and I'm not in the mood."

Without another word, Abel headed for the lunch line.

I didn't bother going after him because, honestly, I was furious. His comment reminded me of how we'd first started talking, when he criticized me on Toughen Up Tuesday.

"Thinks he knows everything," I muttered, stomping down the hall. "Which of us is writing for the advice column? Huh?"

A passing student blinked at me and then kept walking.

My friends had already checked the advice box, so I threw my bag down by my desk and dropped into my seat.

"What's up with you?" asked Tim. "Did you get bit by a voluminous snake?" He smiled but I didn't. "Okay, yikes. I'm out." He turned and faced the front of the classroom.

"Everything okay?" asked V.

I shook my head, but instead of speaking to her, I turned to Heather. "I'm going with you after school. And Madame Delphi better have some good news."

Back to the Future

I may have spoken slightly louder than necessary.

"Uh . . . you're gonna what?" Vanessa stared wide-eyed at Heather, who squirmed in her seat.

"It's no big deal. I just didn't get a complete fortune like you guys, and I want to know what I'm missing."

"Nothing-uh!" V drew out the word and made her thumb and fingers into a zero. "Because it's all a bunch of make-believe." She pointed her pen at me. "And why do you want to waste your money? She's only going to tell you the same thing when she sees you."

I snapped my fingers. "You're right! I should wear a disguise."

Vanessa made an exasperated sound. "That's not what I meant."

"Actually, I think she should go," spoke up Tim.

"What?" V frowned.

"Think about it. If Brooke goes in disguise and gets a completely different fortune, we'll know Madame Delphi's a fraud."

"Oh." The anger in Vanessa's eyes subsided. "That's not a bad idea."

"And if I get the same fortune, this time I can ask how long I'm destined for doom," I said. Then I batted my eyelashes at V. "By the way, I could really use someone's help with my disguise."

Vanessa was quiet for a moment before she nodded. "Okay, I'll do it. But only to prove you wrong. *And* I'm coming with you guys to make sure you don't get swept up in the crazy."

"Oh, yay, this'll be fun!" said Heather. "Tim, do you want to join us?"

I expected him to laugh until soda came out his nose, but instead he nodded. "Sure. I want to meet the infamous Madame Delphi."

He, Vanessa, and I texted our parents to let them know, and Heather texted her *bubbe* to make sure she had room in her car for three more passengers.

We put our phones away just as Mrs. H took her place at the front of the classroom and called for order.

"You've had a day to think about what you'd like to contribute to our *winning* issue"—she emphasized with a smile—"so tell me what you've got."

There were a couple of teams like mine who were waiting for better material to come in, but Stefan held up a huge piece of poster board. He turned it so we could all see the front, which was a mock-up of an article about basketball, complete with a photo he'd taken during a basketball practice that had caught a player midair.

"Nice action shot!" someone said. Stefan nodded his agreement.

"This is the sports team's submission," said Stefan. "I know I said my Adrenaline Dennis piece was going to be the winner, but then I remembered this article. It's about a player who can only see out of one eye."

Several people murmured appreciation.

"Yeah," said Stefan. "The sports team is pretty proud of this piece."

Heather, V, and I glanced at Tim, who shook his head. "First I'm hearing of it."

Mrs. H was polite enough to simply nod, but Mary Patrick said, "You wasted your money on this? You could've just sent me the file."

Stefan blushed but held the poster board even

higher. "I just wanted to make sure everyone had a chance to see it and agree." He swiveled in his seat again so we could all get a glimpse.

Mrs. H glanced at Mary Patrick. "It *is* a good article . . . and a really good photo," she said, putting a checkmark on the board by the sports team. She called on the clubs team last, and I stiffened, thinking of their bid for Young Sherlocks, until they announced they'd chosen to write about the newest clubs of the season.

We broke into our small groups, and I went into Bossy Brooke mode.

"Okay, guys, we only have a few more days to pick what could be our best column ever *and* part of our best paper ever. Make me laugh, make me cry, and make me think."

All four of us were quiet for a while, reviewing advice requests and going over the online ones I'd printed out to share.

"Wow, when people are anonymous, they do

not hold back," said Heather. "'Dear Lincoln's Letters, I can't stop eating dog biscuits. I don't even own a dog!'"

"Sounds rrruff!" said Tim, barking. The rest of us laughed.

"What was Anonymous's question?" asked Vanessa.

"He wanted to know if he's going to die," said Heather, clutching the paper to her chest and making a sad pout. "And he signed it 'Good Boy.'"

"Awww!" said V and I.

"Maybe he's part dog," said Tim. "We should find out and sell his story to the tabloids."

"What is it with you and money lately?" I asked.

"Do you realize how much it costs to be friends with Berkeley Dennis?" he countered.

Heather's jaw dropped. "He makes you *pay* to be his friend? Tim . . ."

He shook his head. "Of course not! It's just

that the kinds of things he likes to do are a little outside my budget."

"Things like what?" Heather pressed.

Tim held out a hand, palm up. "I'll tell you if you give me five dollars."

"No to that," I cut in. "And no, Good Boy isn't going to die from eating dog biscuits. When they make pet food in factories, they actually have humans taste-test it."

My friends all stared at me.

"What?" I could feel my face warming. "It's common knowledge. Everybody knows."

"I didn't know that," said Tim.

"Me neither," said Heather.

"Me neither," said Vanessa. A grin spread across her face. "How did *you* know?"

I sighed and whispered, "My parents had a dog when I was a baby, and I used to eat some of his food, okay?"

Instantly, our corner of the room was filled

with a chorus of "Ewww!" and laughter.

"Did you eat side by side from the same dish?" asked Tim with a gleeful grin. "Or did you get your own bowl of kibble?"

Vanessa slapped her desk and laughed even harder.

"Guys, stop! It was just like baby food!" I said. Then, because they wouldn't stop laughing, I couldn't help starting. "And it gave me a really shiny coat," I added with a giggle.

Heather let out a squeal of laughter and clapped a hand over her mouth when the rest of the class turned to look.

"Okay, shh, shh," I said, putting my finger to my lips. "We have to focus before Mary Patrick comes over here. Sorry, Heather, but a boy who eats dog biscuits isn't award-winning material."

"And Brooke should know as champion of the Westminster Dog Show!" said Tim.

We all cracked up again.

By the time class ended we'd settled on a question for Tim to run in the overall contest from a girl who wanted to know why guys never went for smart girls. After spending time with my friends I was in a better mood, so as soon as the bell rang, I left to find Abel so we could talk.

But he wasn't very interested.

"I walked past your classroom when I finished eating," he said. "I figured you'd be upset about our fight, but when I looked in the window, there you were, laughing like everything was just fine."

I couldn't win with him.

"I'm sorry I wasn't curled up in the corner in a crying heap, but it was just a little fight," I told him. "You were rude and I got over it. I thought you'd be—"

"*I* was rude?" He pointed to himself, wide-eyed. "Brooke . . ." Abel ducked his head and turned away. "Forget it."

"Wait, what?" I tried to grab Abel's arm, but he pulled out of my grasp and kept walking. "Abel!"

Maybe it was time for *me* to start turning in advice questions to Tim.

My stomach twisted as I watched Abel leave, and my forehead wrinkled so much that it was still stuck that way when I met Vanessa and Heather in the girl's bathroom after school.

"What's going on here?" V asked, tapping my forehead with a pencil.

"Are you still worrying about Abel?" asked Heather, who was sitting on the counter next to me. Since she and I were in history together, I'd told her about my brief and confusing encounter. All she could suggest was giving him time to cool off.

"I did like you said," I informed her while Vanessa went to work on my makeover. "But when I went by his locker just now, he mumbled about talking later and left."

"He'll come to you when he's ready," said Heather with a sympathetic smile.

I could feel Vanessa drawing on my eyebrows, but it felt like she was coloring *way* outside the lines.

"If you're making me look like a clown, I will throw a pie at you," I warned her.

"Relax," she said when she was finished. "I'm giving you darker, thicker brows. Auburn eyebrows aren't very common, you know. Come to think of it, neither is auburn hair."

"I already thought of that," I said. I reached for my backpack and pulled out a baseball cap, tugging it onto my head so only my ponytail showed. "We can tuck my hair underneath."

"That'll work," said Vanessa, pulling the cap back off. Then she opened a makeup palette and dipped a makeup sponge in white goo.

"You *are* trying to make me look like a clown!"

I shied away, but she put a firm hand on one of my legs.

"Brooke, stay still! I'm contouring. It's an optical illusion to change the shape of your face." After she applied white to my forehead and cheeks, she switched to a darker shade and rubbed it into my nose and jawline.

"Wow," said Heather while Vanessa worked. "That's amazing!"

"Right?" V asked with a smile. "Katie taught me. Apparently, it's a big thing in California."

With a few more flicks of the wrist, V turned me toward the mirror. "What do you think?"

I was gazing at a stranger . . . a stranger who could predict my every move. When my mouth dropped open, so did hers.

"Whoa," I said. "This is so creepy."

The girl in the mirror agreed.

"And you know what? Let's not go with the baseball cap." V untied the scarf she'd been wearing around her waist like a sash. "Let's go head wrap."

She draped it over my head and tucked my hair underneath before fastening the ends.

The last sign of me was gone.

"Perfect!" I said. "Time to meet Tim."

The three of us found him waiting in the student lounge, and when he saw me, he did a double take.

"Brooke?" He squinted at me and then looked at V. "What did you do, wash her face?"

She and Heather laughed.

"You're lucky I injured my punching hand," I told Tim with a mock scowl. "Are we ready to go?"

It was fun to walk down the hall and see people stare in confusion. And when we got into Heather's grandma's car, she studied me so long she almost swerved into a fire hydrant.

That part wasn't as fun.

"Why the disguise?" she asked.

I couldn't very well tell her the real reason. *You see, a fortune-teller told me I had bad luck, so I'm going to trick her into giving me a different future.* So I settled for "We're doing an exposé for the paper, and I'm undercover."

That answer seemed to satisfy her, and she parked in front of Madame Delphi's.

"Thanks, Bubbe," said Heather. "We'll see you in a—"

She laughed. "You think I'm going to wait out here and let the cold get into my bones? I'm going in too!"

Heather and I exchanged a nervous glance, but Vanessa and Tim couldn't have been happier.

"Yeah, the more the merrier!" said V.

"Maybe you can get your fortune read too," said Tim.

I kicked him as we got out of the car.

"Ow! Calm down. I don't have a biscuit for you, Fluffy."

"Biscuit?" asked Heather's grandmother. "Fluffy?"

"It's a long story," said Heather. She paused and added, "Actually, it's short. Brooke used to eat dog food."

"Hey!" I said. "Nobody else needs to know."

I didn't run up the stairs this time. Not with the way my luck was going. I let my friends go first and then I followed behind, holding the porch railing with my left hand as I went up the steps. Heather opened the door, and we were greeted first by harp music, and then by Madame Delphi.

"Welcome! Welcome!" She looked from Heather to Vanessa and smiled. "You've returned!" Then her gaze took in Tim, Heather's grandma, and me. "And you brought some new friends."

Score one for Vanessa's makeup job.

Heather nodded. "I wanted a full consultation this time," she said. "And my friend . . . uh . . . River"—she pointed to me—"wants one too. It's her first time."

Madame Delphi nodded at me and smiled at V, Tim, and Heather's grandma. "What about the rest of you?"

"I'm the chauffer," said Heather's grandma with a chuckle.

"I just wanted to watch," said Tim.

"Me too," said Vanessa. "And maybe ask some questions."

The expression on her face had gone from friendly to standoffish. I couldn't let her ruin this for me.

"Would it be okay if I went first?" I asked in a high-pitched voice that made Tim snicker. After a lethal look from me, he stopped.

"Sorry," he said. "I just saw the love potions

on sale." He nodded to the merchandise section of the cottage. "Are those your biggest seller? Or is it the instant money . . ." He trailed off and smiled. "Excuse me." Then he double-timed it over to the display.

Madame Delphi held open the door to her inner chamber and beckoned for me to enter. I handed Heather my coat, and she squeezed my hand with a hopeful expression.

I sat in the same chair as before while Madame Delphi closed the door and settled in her own chair.

"Would you like me to take your scarf?" she asked, reaching for it.

"Um . . . I should probably keep it on," I said in my fake voice. "I'm getting over a head cold."

She held up a finger. "I have a special tea for that. And we can read the leaves afterward."

My heart thumped faster as she poured the hot water over the leaves. Then she placed a pack of tarot cards on the table. Without waiting for her command, I started cutting the deck and then selected three of the cards.

"I thought this was your first time," she said with an impressed look.

"Oh, I'm . . . I'm just guessing," I said. "Because they're cards, you know? What else would I do with them?" I let out a high fake laugh.

Madame Delphi gave me a strange look but started flipping the cards I'd chosen. I barely paid attention to the first two, representing my past and my present. In my head I was chanting, *Please no Nine of Swords, please no Nine of Swords.*

Madame Delphi flipped the card holding my future.

The image was of a man lying on his stomach with ten swords sticking out of his back.

CHAPTER
6

Bubble Bubble

"That's it! This session is over!" I picked up the card and tore it in half.

Madame Delphi must not have had many raging clients, because she seemed to have no idea what to do. She leaned back in her chair and blinked repeatedly.

"Your reaction is a little strong," she said.

"The guy had ten swords in his back!" I cried. "That's even worse than the nine swords from last time!"

"Nine swords? Last time?" she repeated.

The door to her inner chamber burst open,

and all three of my friends appeared.

"Brooke! Is everything okay?" asked Heather. "We heard shouting."

Madame Delphi gasped and pointed at me. "You're the redheaded girl who was here on Sunday!" She looked me up and down. "In disguise?"

"So what if I am?" I shot back, pulling off the scarf that covered my hair. "You gave me a lousy fortune with zero good news. I'm a kid! You're supposed to lie and say everything's going to be all right!"

Madame Delphi's face took on its familiar haughty expression. "I only speak what the cards show. If you expect a lie, you've come to the wrong place."

V scoffed. "You mean the *right* place. I watched a TV special about people like you. You read body language and tell people what you think they want to hear."

Even though V was coming to my defense, I

turned on her. "That's crazy. Nobody would ever want to hear they were doomed."

"No," agreed V, "but they might be willing to buy all that junk to get rid of it." She gestured to the gift shop. Then she stepped closer to Madame Delphi. "That's what you were trying to do, right?" She put a hand on Heather's shoulder. "And you knew that if you gave someone who doubted you good news, she'd come back."

Madame Delphi's eyes hardened like twin patches of ice, and she pointed toward the chamber door. "Out. All of you!"

Tim held up a copy of *Millionaire by Midnight* and a dollar. "But I wanted to buy this."

Madame Delphi took the money from him and shooed us into the main room. "Leave me!"

"The book was ninety-nine cents," said Tim. "You owe me a—"

The door to Madame Delphi's inner chamber slammed shut, and my friends and I were left standing there with Heather's grandma snoring on the couch.

"Pretty sure you're not getting that penny." I patted Tim on the shoulder while Heather went to wake her grandma.

"How was it?" Heather's grandma asked, rubbing sleep from her eyes.

"I don't know," said Heather. "I didn't get to go in."

"Sorry," said V, biting her lip. "I didn't mean to ruin it for you, but I couldn't let her keep scaring Brooke."

Heather smiled. "It's okay. You were being a good friend."

They both looked at me and I stared back. "What? I'm still doomed."

"Aww." Heather gave me a sympathetic nod, but V roared in exasperation.

"Are you serious? Brooke, that woman is a

fake!" She gestured to the closed inner chamber.

"She predicted the same future for me twice," I told V with a stoic expression. "And she was right."

"It was a lucky guess!" argued Vanessa.

"Ha!" I pointed at her. "Lucky! See? You do believe in luck."

She rolled her eyes. "It's an expression. There is no good luck or bad luck. Tim, back me up, please!" Vanessa elbowed him, and he glanced up from his book.

"Huh? Oh, yeah. This place definitely smells like old cheese."

Vanessa groaned, and Heather's grandmother cleared her throat.

"Maybe we should finish this conversation outside?" she asked.

"Gladly!" V yanked her coat on and opened the front door, stepping onto the porch. Tim followed, eyes still on the book so that Heather had to guide him down the porch steps.

"But what about my bad luck?" I asked as Heather's grandma put my coat around my shoulders.

She chuckled. "If you don't want bad luck, honey, change it."

She followed my friends outside, but I stopped in the doorway.

Could it be that easy?

"Be right there! I . . . uh . . . dropped something!" I called, heading back into the cottage. I made a beeline for the gift shop and grabbed a book I'd spotted earlier: *Living the Charmed Life*. I put the money for it by the cash register and tucked the book into my sling.

"Brooke?" V called from the porch.

"Yep!" I said, hurrying over.

"I'm sorry I snapped," she said. "I just hate that this woman shook you up so bad."

"No problem," I said. "I'm sure my luck will turn around."

In fact, I was going to guarantee it.

It was almost impossible to be patient and wait to read the book. I couldn't pull it out in the car on the way home, and if my parents saw it, they'd take it and give me another long speech about there being no such thing as luck. So I bundled it in my coat when I got home, saving it for when I could carry it to my room and learn how to change my fate.

I felt a little guilty locking my bedroom door since I never try to keep my parents out, but it was going to be hard to explain what I was up to. Plus, I didn't want to get squirted with a water bottle again.

I settled on the floor with Hammie and Chelsea beside me, and, honestly, I was glad they were there. I'd bought a book on magic from a fortune-teller's shop. At least two horror movies I'd seen started that way. Usually cats could sense evil spirits, but since Hammie was busy attacking my shoelaces and Chelsea was trying to stick her head in my glass of soda, I figured I was okay.

I flipped to the index at the back of the book and found a listing for how to create a good-luck charm.

"Perfect!" I said, turning to the page.

The instructions were pretty simple. All I needed was something white to make a wishing circle, a flame in the center, and an object that I wanted to turn into the good-luck charm.

I grabbed some white socks and arranged them in a circle on the carpet with a pumpkin-scented candle in the middle. I lit the candle with some matches my parents kept in the bathroom, and then I scanned my room for something I could carry in my pocket to give me good luck at all times. Unfortunately, this meant Hammie and Chelsea were out.

"Sorry, guys," I said, scratching Hammie behind the ear.

I settled on the first note Abel had ever given me. It was flat and could fit in my pocket easily. Then I read the words in the book and wafted the paper above the flames, making sure it didn't catch fire. I had just blown out the candle when there was a knock at my bedroom door, followed by a handle jiggle.

"Brooke?" Mom's voice called from the other side. "Why is this locked?"

I scooped up the socks and hid them behind my pillow. "Sorry! I was just changing for bed!"

Shoving the note in my back pocket, I unlocked the bedroom door and pulled it open. "What's up?"

Mom took in my outfit. "I thought you were changing for bed." She sniffed the air. "And what's that smell?"

"I lit a candle but didn't really like the scent," I told her. "And I was about to get ready for bed until you showed up," I said without missing a beat.

"Ah," she said. "Well, I wanted to know if everything was okay. You didn't talk much at dinner, and you left the table in a hurry."

"Lots of homework," I lied.

"What did you and the girls do?" Mom sat on my bed next to the pillow hiding my pile of socks. I walked across the room to distract her.

"Heather wanted to go back to the fortune-teller," I told her, "but Vanessa called Madame Delphi a fake and she kicked us out." It wasn't a lie; I was just leaving out my part of the story.

Mom raised her eyebrows. "Oh my." She shifted on the bed, and the pillow fell into her lap, along with a sock. "What . . ."

I was ready with an explanation, like *I'm making sock puppets for charity!* but Mom smiled at me. "Were you folding your own socks?"

"Uh . . . I was going to," I said, which again wasn't a lie. I *was* going to fold them later.

Mom stood and kissed my forehead. "Look at you, showing responsibility. I'm so proud!" She headed for my bedroom door. "If you want cookies, I'm baking a batch right now. They'll be ready in fifteen minutes." She winked. "I think you can stay up just a little later for that."

"Okay," I said in bewilderment. "Thanks."

She walked out and I just stared after her. That had gone way differently than I expected. Especially the part about the cookies. My parents never made cookies during the week!

I reached back and touched the note in my pocket.

Could my good-luck charm already be

working? Only one way to know for sure.

I picked up the phone and dialed Abel's number. He answered right away, and I said what I'd been thinking all day.

"I know you're upset with me, and I wish we could talk about what I did wrong, because I really don't know. I don't want to fight anymore." I took a deep breath. "So could you tell me what I did wrong please?"

My heart pounded against my chest. I wasn't sure if Abel would push me away again or end things for good, but I took the fact that he didn't hang up as a promising sign.

After a moment of silence he answered.

"It's just . . . sometimes you only think about how things affect you," he said. "And you can be a little bossy."

I was quiet for a moment. "Believe it or not, you're not the first person to say that."

Abel gave an amused snort.

"Look, you're right," I continued. "I *am* a little bossy. But only because I want what's best for the people I care about. I'm sorry. I should trust that you know what's best for you."

"Thanks," he said. "And I'm sorry I didn't tell you what was bugging me, but it was embarrassing. You don't exactly want people knowing that you take orders from the person you're dating."

"Take orders?" I repeated.

"Yeah, like you telling me what to eat or not letting Young Sherlocks get good press because it was bad for you, even though it would've been good for our club."

I winced. "When you put it that way, I sound like a spoiled brat."

"You're not a spoiled brat," said Abel in a softer voice. "You're great."

A happy warmth spread outward from my heart. He still liked me!

"I think *you're* great too," I said, toeing the

carpet. "And Young Sherlocks does deserve to be in the paper. I just have to believe my team can write even better."

"No, no. I want you to win," said Abel. "My interview can wait. I just wanted the choice to be mine."

I nodded even though he couldn't see it. "From now on, this won't be a dictatorship. It'll be a partnership."

"How about a relationship?" Abel asked with a smile in his voice.

"Deal!" I said. "And I'm sorry again. I shouldn't have said anything to begin with. You don't need advice from me on how to eat and exercise. You already know that stuff."

"And so do you," said Abel. "I shouldn't have said I know more than you. I just know different than you. I'm sorrier."

"No, *I'm* sorrier," I said.

Abel laughed. "Okay. I'm willing to let you win this one."

"Oh, you're so kind," I said with a giggle.

I settled back on my bed, and he and I talked for a while until Mom called up that the cookies were ready.

"So are we good?" I asked him.

"Of course," said Abel. "I'll see you tomorrow before school."

When we hung up, I flopped back on the bed and punched the air with my good fist.

Brooke Jacobs was back!

I took the good-luck charm out of my pocket and kissed it.

The next morning I got up before my alarm because Chelsea was patting my face with her paw again. I hugged her close, ignoring her mews of protest and set her gently on the floor. No claws in my hand today! I hummed a Thunder Barrel song while I got ready for school, making sure to slip my good-luck charm into the pocket of my clean jeans, and took the stairs down two at a time.

"Somebody's in a good mood," commented Dad. Then he held up a hand. "Wait. I'm feeling déjà vu, and this time I'm ready to do the Heimlich."

"That won't be necessary," I informed him. "Because my bad luck is gone. For good!"

Mom gave me an amused smile. "Was it the cookies? Because I'd like to take credit for this if I can."

"The cookies were proof of the good luck!" I said, pouring milk into a bowl. As I carried it to the table, a little sloshed over the rim onto the floor, but instantly Hammie was there to lap it up. "See?" I pointed to the cat. "Luck!"

After breakfast, Dad and I grabbed our things

and headed out the door. More snow had fallen during the night, which I kicked to the side with my boots. Something small and shiny went flying, and I bent to pick it up.

"What's this key doing here?" I asked, holding it out to Dad.

His eyes lit up, and he squished my face between his hands. "That's the key for my safe at work! It fell off the ring Monday, and I haven't been able to get into the safe since."

It looked like my good luck was working out for everyone. And at school, it continued. I met Abel in the cafeteria, where he was eating breakfast, and found a dollar someone had dropped. Then in homeroom I was able to help Vanessa with some of her design choices, and she said I had a real eye for fashion, which had definitely never happened before. In math we had a substitute teacher, so I didn't have to learn algebra, and in English I pointed out a mistake in the textbook and earned extra-credit points.

"I swear, you guys, a good-luck charm is the way to go," I told my friends at lunch. "Everything's going right, and my bad luck is a thing of the past." I lifted my slice of pizza, but the cheese and pepperoni were so hot, they slid off the crust and onto my salad.

"Uh-oh," said Heather.

"Look! I invented pizza salad!" I mixed it all together and ate it. "Delicious. Another victory for Brooke."

"Quit rubbing it in," said Tim with a frown. "I haven't been able to take a single bite." He had a napkin tucked into the collar of his white button-up shirt and was trying to eat spaghetti without splashing any sauce on his sleeves. Every time he lifted the fork, noodles would start to slide off and he'd abandon the whole effort.

"Why are you dressed like a businessman?" I asked.

"*Millionaire by Monday* says if you want to be rich, you have to live like you already are," he said.

Vanessa made a face. "And you think rich people wear dress shirts and ties? Have you not seen actors off set?"

"I don't want to be an actor; I want to be a business mogul," Tim said. "With my own private plane."

"How are you living that one?" I asked. "Wait, let me guess." I held my left arm out by my side and made a motor sound with my lips. Vanessa and Heather laughed, but Tim gave me a smarmy look.

"Your airplane only has one good wing." He thumped my right arm with his fingers. "It wouldn't even get off the ground." Then he let out an aristocratic guffaw. "A-haw-haw-haw."

Heather, V, and I stared at him.

"You know, you and Berkeley can probably

do free stuff together," said Heather. "Like have snowball fights or go sledding in the park."

Tim held up a finger. "*Or* we could buy snowball slingers and shields and have *epic* snowball fights! But that costs money. And to make money . . ." He gestured at himself with a flourish.

"I can't believe you're actually following that book's advice," I said.

"How is it any different from you throwing some eye of newt in a bowl and performing voodoo in your bedroom?" Vanessa asked me.

"There was no eye of newt and no voodoo," I said. "It was just a candle and a lucky charm."

Tim grinned. "Do rich people make bad jokes about cereal? Because I really want to."

"What did you use for the charm?" Heather asked me.

I held up the note from Abel. "The first note Abel ever gave me."

"Awww!" she and Vanessa said.

"Ehhh," Tim said, stretching his neck out as he tried to eat the spaghetti with his hand inches above his tray.

"You look like a T. rex," said Vanessa, taking his fork from him. She cut his spaghetti into little pieces.

"So much for living the millionaire lifestyle," I said. "Tim's living the two-year-old lifestyle!"

Heather and V giggled, and Tim stuck his tongue out at me. "Millionaires probably have people who cut up their food for them. And pre-chew it."

"Not a chance," said V. When she was done prepping Lord Timothy's meal, he gave her a grateful smile and carefully scooped some spaghetti up with his fork.

"I think you're both being silly," Vanessa said. "There are no get-rich-quick schemes and no such thing as luck."

I tucked Abel's note back in my pocket. "Suit yourself. But just think how much good luck could help KV Fashions."

"I don't want to do well because I'm lucky," she said. "I want to do well because I deserve it."

"Even if it takes you fifty years?" I asked.

"Even then," said V with a solid nod.

Heather cleared her throat. "Well, I don't have fifty years before my date with Emmett, so . . . Brooke, could you please make me a good-luck charm?"

"Really?" I sat a little straighter in my chair. "Sure!"

"Me too," said Tim.

"Oh for crying out loud," said Vanessa, leaning back and gazing at the ceiling. "Brooke, don't pull them into your delusion."

"It's not a delusion, and I'll prove it," I said. "Something good will happen to me by the end of lunch." I pointed to my watch. "If I'm wrong, we'll all stop being 'silly,' as you call it."

"Good!" said V, crossing her arms. "You've got five minutes." She stared at the clock. So did the rest of us.

One minute and ten seconds later Katie walked over.

"If it isn't the best of the Midwest!" she called. "What's going on, guys?" She saw us all watching the clock and did the same. "Are we trying to turn back time with our minds?"

"Vanessa and I have a bet going," I said.

"Ooh! What kind of bet?" Katie asked.

"Brooke thinks she has magic powers," said Vanessa.

"I don't think that!" I smacked her arm. "You make me sound crazy." I looked up at Katie. "My *good-luck charm* has the magic powers."

Katie's eyes widened. "Really?"

"No!" said Vanessa. "That's the bet."

"Too bad. If you had magic powers, I was

going to ask you to turn these chocolate chip cookies into carrots," she said, holding up a foil package. "You want 'em?"

"Yes," I said with a smug glance at Vanessa. "Yes, I do."

Katie put the cookies on the table, and I held my watch in front of V's face. "Two minutes."

"Ooh!" said Heather. Then she grabbed a cookie.

"Owned!" said Tim.

Vanessa scoffed. "Whatever. Brooke just got—"

"Lucky?" I finished for her, and smiled.

I was going to have fun with this.

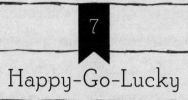

CHAPTER

7

Happy-Go-Lucky

My good luck felt almost like a superpower. Instead of being worried about what might happen next, I was excited. Whatever was coming was guaranteed to be something awesome. And on top of that, I knew that everything would go my way, so I could ask for whatever I wanted.

That's why I strode with confidence into the newsroom and tapped Mary Patrick on the back.

"Uh-oh," said Heather, who had followed me in.

Mary Patrick whipped around and raised an

eyebrow. "This better be important. I was in the middle of gently critiquing someone." Behind her I could see a girl sobbing into a tissue.

"Oh, it is!" I assured her with a confident smile. "I've got some great ideas to help us win the contest. For example, why not make our entry a double issue so we can pack in more content?"

"Because the guidelines restrict us to a standard issue," said Mary Patrick.

"Ah," I said with a nod. "Then how about an issue that also comes with braille dots? So our paper is more accessible."

"Too expensive to print," said Mary Patrick. She gave me a shrewd gaze. "But I like the way you're thinking, Jacobs. Keep up the good work!"

Praise from Mary Patrick. Almost as rare as a unicorn.

I strutted to my desk, beaming at my friends while they gawked at me. Heather had her hand inside a bag of Reese's peanut butter cups, Mary Patrick's favorite.

"I didn't have to throw a single one," she whispered.

"Nah, Mary Patrick's a cinch to deal with." I sat in my chair and leaned back, stretching my left arm luxuriously.

"The other day you said talking to Mary Patrick was like listening to a blender full of rocks," Tim told me.

"That was before I got my good-luck charm." I winked at him. "Speaking of which, don't forget to give me whatever you want to use for yours."

Tim reached into his backpack and pulled out a quarter. "Here you go."

"A coin that's been touched by a thousand people." I wrinkled my nose. "How special."

He shrugged. "If I make a piece of money my good-luck charm, maybe I'll have more good luck with it."

"But what if you accidentally spend the quarter?" asked V.

Tim thought for a moment and took a black marker out of his bag. He drew a T on the tails side. "There."

I pocketed the coin and nudged Heather. "What about you? What's your good-luck charm going to be?"

She grinned sheepishly and put a tube of lipstick on the table. Vanessa gasped and snatched it up.

"Is this lipstick instead of lip *gloss*?" cried V. She hugged Heather tight. "I've never been prouder!"

Heather giggled. "It's what I'm wearing on my date with Emmett. You know, since I promised myself I was going to try new things. I want to be bold and stand out."

"Be bold and stand out," I repeated with a smile. "I like that. And I'll take *that*." I grabbed the lipstick from V. "Heather, you'll have your good-luck charm tomorrow morning. For now, let's get down to business."

We dove into the latest advice requests.

"I've got a good feeling about today," I said. "There's a contest-worthy question right . . . here." I plucked one out of the pile. "'Dear Lincoln's Letters, I want to try out for the swim team this year, and I'm a really good swimmer, but I don't take tests very well, especially when people are watching. I'm afraid I'll fail. Any advice? Sincerely, Swimfan.'"

"That might actually make a pretty good entry," said Heather.

"Sounds like whoever it is could use a good-luck charm," I mused.

"Don't you dare," said V. "Tim, put a new rule in the book. We don't offer magical solutions, only real ones."

"I think that's the strangest rule we've ever

had," he said, reaching into his book bag.

In order to be the best advice columnists we can, my friends and I have compiled a list of things to do and not do for a successful column.

"Give me a little credit!" I said as Tim scrawled the new rule in our book. "I was totally going to throw in some solid advice too."

In fact, I was already crafting the response in my head. The good-luck charm would make Swimfan feel confident *and* fearless.

"What do you think of this for mine, instead of the one about dating a smart chick?" asked Tim. "It's from a guy who wants to date a girl, but her family is rich and his lives in a tiny shack."

"Tim!" Heather gave him a horrified look.

He raised his arms defensively. "His words, not mine!"

"I think it could be a good piece," I said. "Not just for people whose parents make different money, but for different religions or races too.

And you could even mention dating smart girls."
I pounded a fist on the desk. "This is good! All we
need now is a piece for Heather. And remember,
we're not looking for the typical 'My boyfriend
and I are fighting.' We want substance!"

"Yes, Mary Patrick, Junior!" Tim saluted me.

My friends and I sifted through the papers
and emails for a few minutes before Vanessa
picked one out of the pile.

"'Dear Lincoln's Letters,'" she read, "'I know
my best friend is wrong about something, but
she won't listen. I'm afraid it'll only hurt her in
the end. How do I get through to her?'"

I raised an eyebrow at her. "Is it signed 'Confused and Fabulous' in sparkly, purple ink?"

V stuck her tongue out at me. "No, I didn't
write it. But I should've!"

"That would be against the rules." I wagged
my finger.

"This question could work," said Heather.

"Especially if what the best friend is wrong about is something dangerous. Does it say?"

Vanessa shook her head. "But I'll bet it could turn into something dangerous. Especially if her friend is afraid she'll get hurt."

Heather frowned. "Yikes. Should we try and find out who this is?"

"I don't think we can." Vanessa turned the paper so she could see it. "Unless you recognize the handwriting."

None of us did.

"It's probably nothing too terrible," I said.

"I'll make sure it's my piece for the next issue anyway," said Heather.

Vanessa was about to comment when we heard something that had never been heard before: Gil shouting.

"You can't do that!" he hollered at Stefan, who didn't seem the least bit swayed by Gil's words or volume.

"I did some thinking after yesterday, and everyone had a good point," said Stefan. "My basketball photo is amazing, so I'm switching from entering the section contest for sports to the one for photos."

"What about me?" Gil poked himself in the chest. "I already had a photo I was going to enter. A good one!"

Stefan shrugged. "Yours might be good, but mine is great."

Mrs. H hurried over before a real fight could break out.

"Stefan, I have to agree with Gil. You chose to represent sports, so that's what you'll do."

"Have you seen his photos, Mrs. H?" asked Stefan. "So far this week his assignments have been a photo of a snowman-building contest and the new track team."

Instantly I was on my feet. "What's wrong with the track team?"

"The team is fine," said Stefan. "But there's nothing interesting about a bunch of guys dressed in gray, standing in a line with their hands behind their backs." He held up a photo. "Or an image of people building white things on a white background." He held up Gil's other photo.

Vanessa was all set to come to his defense, but he beat her to it.

"There's only so much you can do in a medium that's black, white, and gray," Gil informed him. "Besides, there's plenty of contrast, *and* the important thing in the picture isn't the snow; it's the students."

Mrs. H took the photos from Stefan and looked at them. "On this one, I have to agree with Stefan. These photos are wonderful, but they lack punch and personality." She smiled at Gil. "I know you're capable of so much more."

"Yes, Mrs. H," mumbled Gil.

She turned to Stefan with a raised eyebrow, awaiting his response.

"Fine," he huffed. "I'll stick with sports, but I guarantee those photos of Gil's won't win anything."

"Neither will sports," I spoke up. "Since we're going to win the section submission." I gestured to the advice team.

Yes, I was feeling that lucky.

From the front of the class there was a "Ha!"

I put my hand on my hip. "Something funny?"

Felix stood and faced me. "You really think you can beat everyone, including headline news? We're on the front page for a reason."

"So readers have something to skip when they're looking for sports?" asked Tim.

"Oooh!" said several people.

I nudged him. "Dude, you're supposed to be supporting the advice column, remember?"

"Sorry, but sports is good too," he said.

"But clubs is better than all of them," said their section leader. "We've always got way more exciting news than the rising price of chocolate milk or the football team getting new footballs." She smirked at Tim, who slapped a palm on the desk.

"If I hadn't reported on it, nobody else would have!"

I leaned toward him. "Probably not the best argument."

Tim raised his voice. "I mean—"

But there was no way anyone was going to hear him. The sections were squaring off against one another, talking trash and placing bets. Mrs. H and Mary Patrick fought to restore order, and I just smiled through it all.

"You're not jumping in?" asked Vanessa. "You love fights!"

"Nope. They have to brag because they're not confident enough they can do it." I jerked my thumb at my shouting classmates. "But I know we can, so there's no reason to even argue."

V smiled. "Even though that good-luck charm annoys me, I do like having my confident Brooke back."

"Don't worry," I said with a wink. "I'm not going anywhere."

The bell rang.

"Okay, I may be going somewhere since class is over," I amended.

She and Heather giggled.

The arguing still continued as students flowed into the hall, but their voices were lost among the noise of the crowd. Heather and I made our way to history, where Mr. Costas was holding an Oreo showdown to quiz us on what we'd read the night before. I, truthfully, had read nothing, but as *luck* would have it, I was an incredibly good multiple-choice guesser and won three Oreos.

"You know what this means?" I whispered to Heather while I munched on a cookie. "With my good-luck charm, I never have to study again! Heck, I may never have to do homework either! I can probably just convince my teachers that one of the cats ate it." I chuckled to myself.

Heather furrowed her brow. "Um . . . I don't think I'd count on that, no matter how good your luck is. Plus, don't you want to *earn* your grades?"

"Meh. How much does middle school really matter?" I raised my hand to answer another question. "B!"

"Correct!" Mr. Costas shouted, tossing me an Oreo.

I smirked at Heather and whispered, "Didn't even hear the question!"

She did not share my amusement.

"Oreo?" I asked, offering it to her.

"I'm only taking it because I'm hungry. Not

because I approve," she said, popping it into her mouth. She chewed for a minute and swallowed. "Brooke, I don't think you should rely on your good-luck charm for everything. Maybe for turning a bad situation around, but not for getting out of schoolwork."

"You only say that because you like schoolwork," I pointed out. "If you were bad at it like me . . ."

"Sweetie, you're bad at it because you don't do it," Heather said with a smile.

I held up one of my winnings. "Are we or are we not enjoying cookies because of my good-luck charm?"

She sighed. "We are."

"Do you or do you not want me to make you a good-luck charm?"

"I do, but—"

I held up a hand. "Look, I see what you're saying, but I want to enjoy this good luck for as long

as I can, and I want to share it with my friends."
I leaned closer and whispered, "Wouldn't it be
great if your first date with Emmett was the best
date ever?" I thought about her love of fairy-tale
romance. "With flowers and a horse-drawn carriage?"

She smiled dreamily. "Yeah, it would."

I shrugged. "So your good luck will help you
with dating, and mine will help me with school."

And soccer, I silently added.

Heather giggled. "Yeah, and Tim will probably use his to try and win the lottery."

I sat up straight. "The lottery! Why didn't I
think of that? I can have my parents buy tickets
for me tonight!"

She raised an eyebrow. "I thought you were
saving your good luck for school."

"If I have millions of dollars, I won't have to
go to school," I scoffed.

Heather gave me a tight smile. "Sure. You can

be a sixth-grade dropout instead."

Mr. Costas handed over the last cookie in the pack, and we all groaned. "Sorry, but your other teachers and parents are already going to kill me for the sugar I gave out. But now that I have you full of energy, let's talk Chinese dynasties."

Everyone flipped open their history books while he started lecturing, and my conversation with Heather ended. She wasn't making much sense anyway. Who wouldn't want to take advantage of their good luck all the time?

In fact, I decided I was going to do her a favor. My good luck had to extend to my friends, right? Especially if I was going to do a good deed?

When class ended, I made an excuse to hurry away and tracked down Emmett at his locker.

"Hey, Brooke!" he said with a confused smile. "What's up?"

"Hi! You're going out with Heather on Friday, right?" I asked.

He nodded. "Unless . . . something happened?"

"Nope," I said. "I just wanted to make sure you knew that Heather deserves the royal treatment."

He relaxed and smiled. "Oh, yeah, I was planning on taking her to the movies to see this musical we've both been waiting for."

"How are you getting there?" I asked.

"My mom's dropping us off. I'm not exactly old enough to have a car," he said with a grin.

I shook my head. "No mom. No car. Heather deserves a horse-drawn carriage. And flowers. You'd better be able to give them to her."

Emmett raised an eyebrow. "I will . . . think about it."

I smiled. "Great! Have fun!" I waved and hurried off to my next class, rather proud of myself. Heather was going to have her fairy-tale date, and I was going to be a millionaire. Then I'd buy

Madame Delphi's cottage and turn it into a pizzeria.

But before all that, I still had one thing left to do.

Convince Coach Bly that I was okay to play soccer.

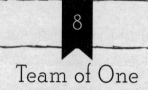
Team of One

"You want a lottery ticket?" asked Mom as she pulled in front of the soccer complex.

"Yes, I've got a good feeling about this one!" I told her.

"Have you also got money to pay for it?" she asked with a smile. "Because I'm not flushing *my* cash away."

I handed her the dollar bill I'd found in the cafeteria. "You've got to spend money to make money, right?"

Mom studied it. "You realize the accountant side of me is screaming, 'Don't do it! Invest!'"

"I am investing," I said, leaning over to give her a one-armed hug. "In my future."

"Your future? What about me and Dad?" she teased as I opened the car door.

"You can live in my guest house," I promised. "See you in a bit!"

"Brooke, wait!" Mom called before I could shut the door. "No playing while you've got that sling on."

"Of course," I said. "No playing with the sling on."

I closed the car door and added, "So I'll just have to take it off."

When I walked into the soccer complex, I peeked around to make sure nobody I knew was in sight. Then I glanced back to see that Mom had left before I unclipped the sling and shoved it in my bag. I hopped up and down a few times as an experiment. My wrist hurt just a tiny bit, but once the adrenaline of the game kicked in, I wouldn't even feel it.

The first thing I noticed when I entered the locker room made my spirits soar even higher: Lacey was nowhere in sight. One less pain to deal with.

"Hey, Brooke! Are you feeling better?" one of the girls asked as I set down my bag. "Oh my gosh, your wrist!"

She and several other girls gathered around me.

"It's okay, it's okay," I assured them. "Only a sprain."

"Phew!" said someone. "With Kayla gone and Lacey sick, we'd be in huge trouble if you couldn't play either."

"Lacey's sick?" I asked.

"Yeah, she has a cold."

That explained why she was sneezing all over the place. But with her out too, that put even more pressure on me. No matter! I had my lucky charm.

I pulled my soccer uniform out of my bag and held it up. "Don't worry, ladies. I'm going to make you proud of your captain! And nobody will be harmed in the process!"

The girls laughed and cheered, changing into their uniforms.

Even though I was the last one into the locker room, I was also the first one out. I grabbed a practice ball and sprinted right up to Coach Bly.

"Brooke!" He reached out for my splinted hand, and it was all I could do not to wince. "What was the verdict?"

"Just a sprain!" I said as cheerfully as possible. "It should be completely healed . . . soon."

A few weeks *was* soon, if you were comparing it to a whole year.

He smiled with relief. "That's what I needed to hear. It looks like Lacey's going to be out for our first game, so you're the only star forward we've got left."

"Who's filling in for her?" I asked.

"Lana," he said.

I sucked air in through my teeth. Lana was fast, which was good, but she couldn't think very well on her feet. That was bad for a spontaneous play change, which sometimes happened in soccer.

Coach looked me in the eyes. "Be honest with me. Are you okay to play?"

"I'm great to play," I assured him.

Except I wasn't. The drills where we stayed in place and juggled the ball or kicked it back and forth were fine, but once I had to start running, my wrist began to ache. I kept the pain off my face, but I couldn't keep it out of my mind. By the time we started running plays, I was so terrified of someone bumping my wrist that I went out of my way to avoid other players. This, unfortunately, meant that I didn't make any attempts to steal the ball, and when I had it, I passed it as quickly as I could to someone else.

After ten minutes of this, Coach blew his whistle and had us take a water break. I tried to join the other girls, but Coach pulled me aside.

"What's going on?" he asked. "Where's my ferocious forward? You're acting like the ball is a bomb you want to get away from."

"Sorry," I said. "I think I'm just a little spooked after what happened yesterday with Lacey."

Coach's worried expression eased. "That was a freak accident. As long as you keep your eyes on where you're going, you'll be fine."

I nodded. "You're right. I'll get my head in the game."

Coach smiled. "Good. Because I've got a new play for us to run."

One of the other girls called him over, and he put his clipboard on the bench to go assist. "Excuse me."

"Sure," I said, taking a seat to fix my laces.

I glanced at the clipboard and saw that the top page was the new play. I paused in tightening my shoelaces.

If I could memorize this play, I could predict the other team's moves and execute it perfectly. No chance of anyone bumping into me because I'd stay out of their reach.

Grabbing the pen off Coach's clipboard, I jotted a quick sketch of the moves on my palm. Then I disappeared into a bathroom stall of the locker room . . . the only place I could stare at my hand in peace. After studying the play for a couple minutes and picturing my part, I returned to the pitch just as Coach blew the whistle to resume practice.

"I've drawn up a new play that I think will get us some goals this weekend. Everybody gather around."

We all huddled close as he explained, and I

nodded along with everyone else, even raising my hand to ask a question so he wouldn't get too suspicious when I aced it the first time out.

"Let's give it a whirl!" Coach said, clapping his hands. We took our positions on the field, and he blew the whistle.

I'm not gonna lie; I deserved both an ESPY *and* an Academy Award for my performance. As soon as that ball reached my feet, I was on the move, zipping past midfielders. I could've shot the goal myself, but I figured it would be better for Coach to see me as a team player, so I passed to Brin, who almost didn't see it coming.

Goal in under a minute.

The girls on my team cheered, and Coach clapped his hands.

"Nicely done, Jacobs! Let's run it again!"

The ball was re-set and we ran the play, but this time the other team was better prepared.

Luckily I'd expected it, and, in addition to Coach's original play, I'd thought of another escape route that would work. I juggled the ball around a defender and took the goal shot myself. It struck the net with a satisfying swish.

My team cheered again, while the opposing team gave me murderous looks.

"Maybe we should just call this play The Brooke," said Coach jokingly.

I was practically walking on air. The pain in my wrist was totally worth it.

"Let's run it again!" he shouted. "Midfielders on defense, I don't want that ball getting past you this time."

Unfortunately, they must have all left their good-luck charms at home, because I swept right through, passing to Jenny this time, who scored our third goal in the first ten minutes. Coach worked with the defense to point out weak spots, but because he was doing it out loud, I was able to avoid those spots, and we made yet another goal.

But . . . this time, it wasn't as satisfying.

While I liked winning, I didn't like winning easily. And now I understood what Heather had said about school. She wanted to earn her good grades, and I wanted to earn my victory. These girls were practically handing it to me, and I knew exactly why.

I was a team of one.

It was me driving the ball down the field, me making the goals. Yeah, I was passing to the other girls, but they were really just an extension of me.

If Lacey were there, she would've been all over the ball, and I would've had to work with her to make the goals. But my good luck was *so* good, nobody could step to me. Even on plays we'd practiced a hundred times. Toward the end, I was intentionally not playing as well just so other girls could have a chance. For the second time in a row, Coach called me over.

"You started doing better, but now you're giving away some easy shots," he said. "What's going on?"

I couldn't stop the truth from coming out. "It's too easy. I feel like I'm playing against U8s, so I thought I should take it down a notch."

Coach shook his head. "Don't do that. They can't learn if they aren't challenged. Just play like yourself. We've got to train the rest of these girls up."

I gave a firm nod and returned to the pitch. This time I didn't hold anything back. Even though Coach said I was helping the team, they sure didn't look like they appreciated it. If it wasn't for my good-luck charm, they probably would've trampled me with their cleats.

At the end of practice, we all went into the locker room to change, and I could practically feel the sweat on my forehead freeze from all the icy stares I was getting.

"What?" I asked. "I told you guys I was going to prove I was a good captain, and I did."

"Yeah, but you made the rest of us look bad," said one of the defenders. A couple of her teammates murmured their agreement.

"No," said a girl on my team, "you guys made *yourselves* look bad."

I held up my hands to quiet the girls, and several of them gasped. One girl screamed.

"What?" I glanced down at my right hand. It was bright purple. "Augh!"

Brin grabbed my good arm and dragged me out of the locker room. "Coach Bly! Coach Bly!"

He looked up from where he was throwing soccer balls into a bag. "What's wrong?"

Coach took one look at me and hurried over. "Brooke, I thought you said you were okay to play."

"Well, mentally I am," I said, wincing as he unstrapped the splint. My wrist was even more swollen than it had been the day before. "Uh-oh."

Coach Bly turned to Brin, who looked like she either wanted to throw up or scream. "Go to the first aid kit and get some ibuprofen and a cold pack."

She nodded and ran away.

"She's getting faster," I commented with a weak smile.

Coach pointed at me. "You are not playing soccer until I get an official note from your doctor saying it's okay."

"It's not that bad," I said. "Look, my hand is turning back to its normal color." I showed him. "Besides, you can't spare losing another starter. You said so yourself."

He gave me a tight smile. "I think we can make an exception in this case."

Brin reappeared with the ibuprofen, cold

pack, and a bottle of water. Several of the other girls were with her.

"Thanks," I said, taking the ibuprofen and bottle of water from her while Coach snapped the disks in the cold pack to make it freeze.

"Coach, if Brooke is out too, what are we going to do?" asked Brin.

"You're going to play your best," he said, placing the cold pack on my wrist.

"But what if our best isn't good enough?" asked Lana, Lacey's replacement.

"It will be," I said. "I'll come up with some tips for you and Brin and whoever Coach chooses to replace me." I looked up at him, and he thought for a moment.

"Allison," he said, naming another of our second-string forwards.

She was fast, had good reaction skills, but wasn't a very aggressive player. Nevertheless, I smiled at Allison, who was in the crowd of girls.

By the time Mom picked me up, the swelling in my wrist had gone down enough for Coach to put the splint back on, and I sheepishly pulled my sling out of my bag and let him help me put my arm through it.

"Does she have to know about today?" I asked with pleading eyes.

Coach clapped me on the back. "I wouldn't be a good coach *or* a good person if I didn't tell her to keep an eye on you."

Mom was kind enough not to fly into a rage in front of him, but as soon as we were on the road, she let me have it.

"How dare you disobey your father and me! I can't believe you would do something so dangerous! Don't you have any regard for your own safety?"

Apparently good-luck charms do not work on angry moms.

I was smart enough to stay quiet until she'd

finished with "Do you have anything to say for yourself?"

"I love soccer," I told her. "And I care about my team. I didn't want to let them down."

For some reason, that seemed to calm her.

Mom sighed. "Sweetie, that's admirable, but sometimes you have to put yourself first."

I thought back to practice and frowned. "Not when it comes to soccer. People don't like that."

"What do you mean?" she asked.

I told her about my winning streak and she frowned too.

"Brooke, that's cheating."

I gaped at her. "No, it's not!"

"You looked at the coach's playbook," she said. "Before anyone else had a chance to. That was an unfair advantage." She pulled into our driveway. "Also known as cheating."

"Let's just agree to disagree," I said, getting out of the car.

Mom followed me. "That's what people say when they know they're wrong but won't admit it."

"It wasn't an unfair advantage," I argued. "Coach left it where anyone could see it. I just chose to be proactive." I walked inside and shrugged off my coat. "Dad would take my side."

"I'd take your side on what?" called a voice from the kitchen.

I froze and looked at Mom, who shrugged.

"Parental Scolding, round two," she said.

Either Dad knew Mom had already done enough yelling for the both of them or thought I'd learned my lesson, because when he found out I'd been playing, he simply said, "Your mother's right. And you can say good-bye to your allowance this month."

"Oh, she won't have anything to spend it on since she's grounded anyway." Mom gave me a huge smile and a side squeeze.

Maybe there was a special good-luck charm just for parents.

"Well, since I've got nowhere to go and no money to spend, I'll be up in my room," I said. "Let me know when dinner's ready."

"Cheer up, honey!" Mom called as I trudged upstairs. "Your lottery ticket might be a winner!"

As I closed the door, I heard Dad asking Mom, "You bought her a lottery ticket?"

Chelsea and Hammie were curled up on my bed when I opened the door to my room but jumped down to greet me. Hammie sniffed at the lipstick and quarter I placed on the carpet.

"Sorry, Hamm. It's nothing you'd be interested in."

I arranged the socks in a circle on the floor. Then I placed my pumpkin candle in the center and lit it.

Since Heather needed the most luck, I waved

her lipstick over the flame first. Then Tim's quarter. I even added a little something for V in case she changed her mind.

Shortly after I blew out the candle, Mom yelled up that dinner was ready.

We had just settled at the table and I had a mouthful of bread when Dad cut into his meat and said, "So I walked past your room and heard you talking to yourself earlier." He speared his meat and studied it thoughtfully. "It sounded like you were saying a spell, but I thought your witches' coven only met on Thursdays."

I groaned and lowered my napkin.

"Aw, tell them we said hi," added Mom with an exaggerated smile. "If you're not busy turning princes into frogs."

I rolled my eyes and swallowed my bread. "You guys are hilarious."

"Actually it sounded like she was asking for good luck," said Dad. He tilted his head to one side. "How's that working out, sunshine?"

I scowled at him. "Can we not?"

Mom and Dad grinned at each other.

"Okay, we're sorry," said Dad. "How's that algebra coming? Are you ready for the quiz tomorrow?"

"Absolutely," I said.

I wasn't, but I figured my good-luck charm would take care of that. My good-luck charm also got me out of doing the dishes since I only had one usable arm.

"Just go finish your homework," said Mom. "I'll take care of the dishes."

I didn't bother with homework. Instead I called Abel, and we chatted about his track practice and my soccer practice. Then I called V, and we talked more about KV Fashions and some ideas she'd come up with.

"A fashion show at school!" she told me.

"That sounds awesome," I told her. "Do you

think they'd let you do it?"

"Katie and her parents are good friends with Principal Winslow, remember? It should be easy!"

"Yay!" I said, glancing at the good-luck charm I'd made for her. "When did you guys decide on that?"

"When Katie came over a couple hours ago to watch a fashion show," V explained.

I smiled to myself. My friends didn't even need to have their good-luck charms with them for them to work! I was kind of awesome. "You're welcome."

"Huh?"

"I mean well done!"

"Thanks!" said V. "Well, I should probably get off the phone and work on newspaper stuff."

I sighed. "Yeah, me too."

That I knew wouldn't take care of itself. I hung up with V and lay back on my bed, trying to think of ways to make the paper more interesting. How did Vanessa make fashion interesting? I pictured her book of designs, with its tabbed sketches and bold colors. Thinking about bold colors made me think of Heather's lipstick. Then I started jotting ideas. My friends were brilliant without even knowing it. Even Tim. Although his response would most likely be "Duh."

I pulled Abel's note from my pocket and kissed it. "You've done it again!"

Once I'd finished my ideas for Mary Patrick, I went to work on my letter for the kid who lacked confidence. After seeing Brin and Jenny on the field, the inspiration flowed. I talked about believing in yourself and how nobody was perfect and it was better to try and fail than to never try at all. My advice was heartfelt and uplifting and motivational.

If the *Lincoln Log* didn't win the newspaper contest, it wouldn't be because of me.

At bedtime, Mom knocked on my door to say good night.

"Did you get all your schoolwork done?" she asked as I settled down under the covers.

I nodded. "And I came up with ways to make the newspaper better for a contest we're entering."

"That's great!" She beamed and squeezed my hand. "And it's all thanks to Brooke's brain." She kissed my forehead. "No luck needed."

"Yeah . . . ," I said noncommittally. "Mom, why don't you want good luck to be real?"

She smiled. "It's not that I don't want it to be real. I just don't think people should rely on it to get what they want. And I definitely don't think they should use it to justify doing the wrong thing, like peeking at the coach's playbook." She poked my stomach.

I laughed. "I won't do it again, I promise."

"Good. Sleep tight, honey." She gave me

another kiss on the forehead and walked away.

"Mom?" I sat up a little. "If you ever want me to make you a good-luck charm, I will."

Her expression softened. "I already have one. Her name is Brooke."

Mom turned off the light and closed the door.

CHAPTER

9

Karma

The next morning in the student lounge I gave V the good-luck charm I'd made for her. It was a shiny brass button.

"And not just any button," I pointed out when I put it in her palm. "This is the button we found when we were in first grade. Remember?"

V smiled at it fondly. "We both thought it was solid gold and tried to figure out how to spend our riches."

"Did someone say riches?" Tim popped up from behind a chair, and V and I both jumped.

"What are you doing back there?" I asked.

"*Millionaire by Monday* says you should always bet on yourself, so I bet some guy I could make a basket into the trash can and I lost. Now he's trying to collect."

V and I looked at each other and cracked up. Tim shushed us.

"It's not funny! I don't carry that kind of cash!"

I reached into my pocket and pulled out the quarter he'd given me. "Well, here. Hopefully this will bring you some luck."

"Aw, sweet!" Tim cupped a hand around his mouth. "Hey, Alex, I have that money I owe you!"

I gave him a bewildered look. "All you owed him was a quarter?"

"Yeah." Tim nodded to a guy and flipped him the coin.

"But you said you don't carry around that kind of cash," pointed out Vanessa.

"Yeah, because usually I spend it on soda," he said. "Thanks, Brooke. That quarter *was* lucky."

"No problem," I said as V and I started laughing again.

When Heather walked up a minute later, Vanessa tugged on her arm. "You wouldn't believe what just happened!"

Heather frowned. "You're not going to believe what happened to me either. Emmett cancelled our date."

Instantly, Vanessa and I were no longer in laughing moods.

"What?" I asked. "Why?"

Heather turned to me. "Because you made him."

"Me?" I squeaked.

"Hold up, hold up." Vanessa waved her hand in the air. "Brooke would never do something like that."

"Never!" I agreed.

"Did you talk to Emmett about the date?" Heather asked.

I cringed. "I mean . . . never on purpose."

V shook her head. "Oh, Brooke. What did you do?"

"She made me sound like a diva," said Heather, dropping onto the couch. "Apparently, I won't date a guy without a horse-drawn carriage and flowers?" She raised an eyebrow at me.

I took a seat next to Heather and squeezed her hands. "I only had the best intentions. The best. I didn't know he'd give up so easily."

"Can you blame him?" asked Heather. "This was only our first date! Geez, Brooke, did you have to get involved?"

"Yes! You're one of my best friends," I said. "And one of the nicest people I know. I just wanted to make sure you were treated like the princess you are."

Heather leaned back and sighed. "Well, much like Cinderella, this girl won't be going to the ball."

"Yes, you will! I'm going to fix this." I stood and immediately sat back down with one tug from Heather.

"No," she said firmly. "He's made his choice. And I don't want to go out with a guy who lets other people change his mind for him." At the worried look on my face, she attempted a small smile. "I'll be fine."

But it didn't make me feel any better. My good-luck charm should've ensured the horse-drawn carriage, the flowers, and a happily ever after!

"I'm really sorry," I said. "I thought I was helping." I reached into my book bag and pulled out the lipstick. "I guess it's a little late for this, huh?"

"Heh. Yeah." Heather managed a real smile this time. "But who knows? Maybe I'm supposed to save it for a date with someone else." She put the lipstick in her bag. "I'll see you guys later, okay?"

She got up and headed for the exit, leaving V and me to stare after her.

"I feel so horrible," I said, sinking into the couch.

"Hey, you were only trying to help," said V, bumping my shoulder.

I shook my head. "I just don't understand it. My—" I reached into my back pocket for my good-luck charm but felt only fabric.

My good-luck charm was missing.

"Are you okay, or is this some new dance?" V asked as I stood and patted down the pockets of my jeans and hoodie.

"I can't find my good-luck charm!" I said, ripping my backpack open and rummaging through it.

"Here, you can have mine." She offered me the button, but I shook my head.

"It doesn't work like that." I pulled my cell phone out of the side pocket of my bag and dialed home.

"Hey, sweetie," Mom answered. "Did you

forget your homework?"

"Worse! I forgot my good-luck charm!" I lamented. "Can you bring it to me?"

The gentle tone in Mom's voice disappeared. "Brooke, you can't be serious. I've got clients all day. I'm not driving up there to drop off some lucky rabbit's foot."

"It's not a rabbit's foot; it's a piece of paper," I said.

Silence from the other end.

"Mom?" I checked to make sure she was still there.

"Um . . . where was the last place you had it?" she asked.

I breathed a sigh of relief. She was going to do it! "The pocket of my warm-ups last night. It should still be there."

Mom breathed through her teeth. "It *was* there. Now it's all over the inside of the washing machine."

"What?" I cried loud enough for everyone in the student lounge to look my way.

"Everything okay?" asked V.

I shook my head and walked to a quiet corner of the room. "What do you mean it's all over the washing machine?" I hissed into the phone.

"I needed extra clothes to fill out a laundry load, so I threw in your clothes from yesterday," said Mom. "I didn't think to check the pockets. I'm sorry, sweetie!"

I clapped a hand to my forehead. "No wonder my day's off to a bad start!"

"Brooke, I've told you before, luck has nothing to do with it," said Mom.

"Yeah, that'll be a great inscription for my tombstone," I muttered. "Talk to you later."

I trudged back to V, who was now sitting with Gil.

"Uh-oh," she said when she saw me. "Bad news?"

"My good-luck charm is gone forever," I said. "Bad Luck Brooke is back." I held my hands out like barriers. "You may want to keep a safe distance."

Vanessa elbowed Gil, who said, "Uh . . . that's not true! When I was doing the horoscope, I saw that you're in for happier days."

"Really?" I perked up but then narrowed my eyes. "Wait. What's my sign?"

Gil wrinkled his forehead. "Capri . . . gemi . . . taur . . . ies?"

Vanessa patted his back. "Nice try."

He shrugged. "I didn't expect her to call my bluff."

V turned to me. "Not that I support this in any way, but why don't you just make a new good-luck charm?"

I snapped my fingers. "Of course!"

The bell rang, and we said good-bye to Gil in the main hall. On the way to homeroom, I saw

Mary Patrick coming out of the girl's bathroom.

"Hey, I'll catch you later," I told Vanessa, and changed course to catch up to Mary Patrick. She glanced at me as I fell into step beside her but didn't utter so much as a hello.

"I came up with some great ideas to make the *Lincoln Log* stand out!"

"It doesn't matter," said Mary Patrick.

I tried again. "Well, don't turn them down until you've heard them. See—"

Mary Patrick stopped in the middle of the hall, causing a pileup of angry kids behind us. "It doesn't matter because we're not entering."

That was when I noticed her eyes were blotchy and her nose was pink.

Mary Patrick had been crying. And as we stood there, she looked ready for round two.

I grabbed her arm and pulled her to the side of the hall. "What's wrong? What happened?"

"Mrs. H got really upset because everyone

was fighting over which section was best, and she said this contest was just going to drive us all apart." The longer she spoke, the more Mary Patrick's voice quavered. "This was my last year to enter, and I won't even get a chance." Mary Patrick burst into tears.

I closed my eyes and leaned against the wall.

Here was something else that was my fault. This wouldn't have happened if I'd stayed out of Gil and Stefan's argument and hadn't bragged about how much better my team was.

I opened my eyes and said, "Mrs. H should still let us compete in the overall competition."

"She says if we don't win, each section will blame another."

"If we don't win," I mumbled. "Thanks for the confidence boost, Mrs. H."

"I know, right?" Mary Patrick sniffled and pulled a tissue out of her pocket.

"Well, with my ideas I think we've really got a

shot at taking this contest. We just have to convince Mrs. H to let us enter."

"Good luck with that," said Mary Patrick.

I winced. That seemed to be the theme of the week.

I made it to homeroom right before the bell rang and shared my dilemma with Vanessa.

"Shoot!" She banged a fist on her desk. "I already had something in mind for that money too."

"You might still get it," I said. "If I can convince Mrs. H we're one big, happy family. Do you have a box of matches?"

V's eyes widened. "What exactly are you planning?"

"Nothing dangerous," I assured her. "I just need to make another good-luck charm. All this bad luck is starting to snowball."

"Oh. Well, sorry, I don't." V smiled at me. "But I'm sure it can't get much worse."

Needless to say, it did.

In math I had an algebra quiz. I'd expected my good-luck charm to help me ace it, but since the charm was destroyed, it was up to me and my math skills to get things done. I worked all the way up until the bell rang and ended up making random guesses for the last few problems. When I handed in my paper, the teacher frowned.

"Ms. Jacobs, you answered 'true' for question eight."

I cleared my throat. "I was going to go with 'false'—"

"Which would have also been wrong," she said, "since this was a multiple-choice question."

"Ah. Well, true and false *are* more than one choice, so technically . . ." I pressed my lips together as her red pen turned my paper into the site of a math massacre. Then she scrawled a note at the bottom, followed by a line.

"Please take this home to your parents and

have them sign on the line," she said. Then she reached into a desk drawer and pulled out a laminated card. "I'll expect to see you in here Monday during homeroom for tutoring."

I hung my head and put the card and quiz inside my math book.

"That bad already?" asked Abel when I ran into him in the hall.

I opened my math book and showed him.

"Ouch. Looks like you'll have to study harder next time," he said.

"Yeah. I guess I can't count on good luck for everything."

Abel laughed loudly. "Are you serious? You thought you could rub a rabbit's foot and get an A?"

"It wasn't a rabbit's foot! Why do people keep thinking that?" I frowned. "My good-luck charm was the first note you ever gave me."

"Aww." Abel squeezed my hand. "Really?"

I smiled despite my situation and squeezed back. "Of course. It's special to me."

"And you're special to me." Abel pulled away. "I can help you with algebra this weekend if you want."

"Thanks," I said. "Maybe if I can show my math teacher I've improved, I won't have to go to tutoring every day. But for now, I have to get to PE."

"I hope your day gets better!" Abel called as we parted ways.

The gym was set up with a line of about twenty balls at half-court, and I remembered that it was Dodgeball Day. That lifted my spirits a little. Until the PE teacher told me I'd have to sit it out.

"But the balls are made of foam!" I told her. "They don't even hurt."

"Sorry, kiddo," she said at my crestfallen

expression, "but I don't think you should play. You can help me referee, though!" she continued, trying to make it sound exciting.

"I guess," I mumbled.

She handed me a whistle and pointed out the best judging spot.

"Watch for kids who get tagged out but try to stay in," she said. "And for kids who claim they tagged someone out but didn't."

I nodded and walked to the other end of the court while my classmates ran out to be assigned to teams.

"Hey! How come Brooke isn't playing?" asked Berkeley Dennis once the teams had been decided.

I held up my arm and pouted. "I'm not allowed."

"But the balls aren't hard." He spoke to the PE teacher now. "And we won't aim for her arm."

The PE teacher shrugged. "Sorry."

"Why do you care so much anyway?" I asked Berkeley.

He grinned mischievously. "Because last time you said you could take on the entire class. I wanted to see if it's true."

Several kids laughed, and the PE teacher blew her whistle. "Everyone to your places!"

The other kids bolted for opposite ends of the court and huddled together to talk strategy until the whistle blew a second time. Instantly, the tension in the room increased as the two teams faced each other.

"Charge!" the teacher yelled.

With various battle cries and shrieks, the kids ran for midcourt, where the balls were lined up. The more daring kids grabbed them while the timid kids stopped halfway and backed up for safety. It was difficult to keep up with the flurry of action, but I caught several kids breaking the rules and sent them off the court.

Then the coach blew the whistle and uttered the most dreaded of all dodgeball words: "No lines!"

The court was now completely open and there was no border to protect the active players.

Or as it turned out, the temporary referee.

"Now!" cried Berkeley.

Eleven kids, dodgeballs in almost every hand, formed a massive half circle and closed in on me.

"Wait! I'm not even playing!" I cried as they surged forward. The PE teacher blew her whistle, but nobody paid attention.

"Remember, no arm shots," Berkeley said to his teammates. "Brooke, you might want to put your wrist behind your back."

This was really going to happen.

Well, I wasn't going down without a fight.

I picked up a ball and grinned at Berkeley. "You're going to regret this," I said, hiding my injured wrist. There was a pattering of footsteps behind me, and Katie appeared by my side.

"Don't worry, Brooke! I'll protect you!" she cried, waving the remaining half of a ball in one hand.

"Where's the other half?" I asked.

She winked at me. "Won't need it."

"Let's get 'em!" cried Berkeley, and he and his friends unleashed a flurry of foam.

But they were no match for a girl with one good arm and a girl with half a dodgeball.

Katie used her half ball as a shield to knock away attacks while she flung fierce dodgeballs with her other hand. She aimed at the feet of her enemies and they had to dance to avoid getting knocked out. I used my good arm and stomach to catch balls thrown my way and then passed them to Katie to use. When Berkeley, the last opponent standing, was taken out, a cheer went up from the other students . . . followed by him being escorted to the principal's office for starting trouble.

"That still wasn't the whole class!" Berkeley called over his shoulder.

"I'll rematch you any day!" I shouted back.

He grinned and gave me a thumbs-up.

I turned to Katie and hugged her. "Thanks for having my back. You were awesome!"

"You were pretty awesome too!" she said with a grin. "I wish I'd had a camera at the end."

"I needed that win after all the bad luck I've had lately," I confided. "I messed up Heather's date with Emmett, I messed up the newspaper's chance to compete, I failed an algebra quiz, and I almost got my butt handed to me in dodgeball."

Katie whistled. "Wow. That's a lot."

"I've really got to make another good-luck charm. Do you have any matches?" I asked, miming lighting one.

"No . . ." She gave me a strange look. "I don't

start a lot of fires at school. But you could check in the science lab."

Lunch hour was the only time I could be sure the sixth-grade classrooms would be empty, so while everyone raced to the cafeteria, I raced to the lab with another one of Abel's notes.

Feeling a bit like a high-tech spy, I grabbed a flint lighter and went in search of a Bunsen burner. They appeared to be locked away, but I found the right keys in the teacher's desk. I'd just opened the cabinet and grabbed a burner when I heard someone clear her throat.

"What are you doing in here?" asked the teaching assistant.

I held up the burner and smiled. "Science?"

She pointed to the exit and smiled. "Principal."

10

New Perspective

Five minutes later I was in the principal's waiting area. I sat there for half an hour, doing my best to ignore the kids walking by and glancing at me through the window. At one point, Heather and Vanessa appeared, gesturing for me to pick up my cell phone.

What happened? V texted in a group message. We heard you blew up the science lab!

I shook my head and texted back. I was trying to make another charm to get rid of my bad luck. Turns out I'm the bad luck.

Heather and Vanessa gave me pitying looks,

and Heather's fingers flew across her phone.

If that's true, then bring it on. I will live with Bad Luck Brooke every day!

Vanessa read what Heather had typed and smirked before sending her response.

Yeah, she already puts up with me pretty well!

I laughed out loud and clapped a hand over my mouth.

How do you do it, V? I texted back. How do you stay so happy even when things go so wrong?

Vanessa thought for a moment and answered with a smile.

Because I choose to.

"I wish I was more like you," I said out loud.

Principal Winslow emerged from his office and appeared in the doorway of the waiting area. As soon as he saw me and my friends texting one another, we all lowered our phones.

"Visiting hours are over, ladies," he said loud enough for them to hear through the window. To me he added, "Your parents just arrived."

Heather and V waved and scurried away.

The door to the waiting area opened, and my parents walked in. I stepped between them and Principal Winslow before he could even say hello.

"I am so sorry," I told Mom and Dad. "I know I messed up."

"What were you thinking?" asked Mom. "Principal Winslow called and said you'd been going through someone else's things!"

"You know better," Dad added.

I nodded. "I was trying to make a good-luck—"

I didn't even get all the words out before both my parents started groaning. Principal Winslow ushered us all into his office and closed the door.

"Did she do any damage?" Dad asked Principal Winslow.

"Thankfully, the teaching assistant caught

Brooke before that could happen," he said. "But even so, we can't take this lightly. We're going to have to suspend Brooke for the afternoon."

"What!" I cried, getting up.

Mom pushed me back down. "We can accept that."

I couldn't. I'd never been in trouble at school in my whole life! I got Good Citizen awards every year!

"Please, Principal Winslow." I clasped my hands together. "I'll clean beakers or pick up trash outside or help the lunch lady. But don't kick me out of school!"

"We're not kicking you out of school, Brooke," he said in a calm voice the opposite of mine. "It's just an afternoon suspension. And normally it would be longer"—Principal Winslow was talking to my parents now—"but since Brooke isn't usually a troublemaker, we'll be lenient this time." He nodded to me. "Consider yourself lucky."

"Yeah, not the best choice of words for this kid," said Dad, reaching over to shake Principal Winslow's hand. "Thank you for your time."

Mom nudged me. "Let's grab your school-work."

"But—"

"Up, Brooke."

I got to my feet. "Can I go by myself while you guys wait in the car? This is embarrassing enough as it is."

Mom and Dad looked at each other, and Mom nodded. "Okay, but you've got five minutes. No stopping to chat with your friends."

"I promise."

Instead I stopped to chat with Mary Patrick. "Here are my ideas for how to improve the paper," I said, handing her a list. "At least show them to Mrs. H and ask her if I can have a chance to prove the entire staff deserves this."

"Shouldn't you tell her yourself?" asked Mary

Patrick, taking the paper.

"I have to go." I glanced at the clock. "Just . . . please."

"Okay," she said with a nod.

I ran out to the car, where Mom and Dad were waiting, and hopped in.

"Thanks. And again, I'm so sorry. If I'm grounded for the rest of the month, I understand. Although, if I could get time off for soccer games . . . they really need me."

"We're not grounding you," said Mom as Dad pulled away from the school.

I wrinkled my forehead. "You're not? I just . . . get to leave school early?"

"Not quite," said Dad. He turned at the intersection leaving the school, but instead of going right, he turned left and sped up.

"We're not going home?" I peered out the window. "Where are you taking me?" I met Dad's eye in the rearview mirror and gasped. "Are you selling me to the circus?"

Dad turned to Mom. "You've got to stop letting her watch those made-for-TV movies."

We pulled into a strip mall, and Dad parked in front of a store called the Sweet Life. The windows were decorated with pastel cake boxes and cupcake appliqués stuck to the glass.

"I thought we could sit and have a serious talk about what's bothering you," said Mom. "With no teasing and no joking."

I smiled at her. "I'd like that."

Dad held open the door to the bakery, and it was like walking into a warm hug. The air smelled of chocolate, vanilla, and sugar, and there were bakery ovens tucked behind the counter with windows lit so we could see the cakes rise. We all ordered our cupcakes and hot drinks and took a table by the window.

While Mom stirred sugar into her coffee, she spoke. "Your dad joked the other day about us going to a seer, but when I was in high school, I really did visit a psychic."

I looked up from the whipped cream I was slurping off my cocoa. "You did?"

Mom nodded. "And she told me to marry my high school sweetheart."

"But you grew up in New York." I pointed at her and glanced at Dad. "And you grew up in Seattle."

He smiled. "That's right."

Mom brushed my hair back. "Honey, I didn't take the psychic's advice, because in my heart I knew it wasn't the right thing to do. I chose a different path, and when your father moved to New York for college, we met and . . ." She held her arms open. "You know the rest."

"If your mom had followed the psychic's advice, I wouldn't be sitting here," said Dad. "And neither would you." He tweaked my good arm, and I grinned.

"So everything turned out okay," I said. "Or . . . great, I should say." I pointed to myself, and my parents laughed.

I felt myself warming inside, and it wasn't just because of the cocoa.

I liked the idea of being in charge of my own future, of being able to make it whatever I wanted.

"So what's got you so confident you're cursed now?" asked Dad.

The funny thing was . . . I didn't feel nearly as sure as I had.

"I guess because I messed up Heather's date," I said. "He cancelled on her because of me."

Mom clucked her tongue. "Poor Heather! Was she really mad?"

I shook my head. "She knew I meant well, so luckily—"

I stopped when I realized what word I'd used, and my parents grinned at each other.

Dad leaned toward me, chin resting on his hands. "Luckily? But I thought you were doomed."

Mom elbowed him. "We promised not to tease." To me she said, "What else happened?"

"I did pretty badly on an algebra quiz." I lowered my gaze to the table. "Because I didn't study."

"We can help you with that in the future," said Dad.

I glanced up. "Actually, Heather and Abel said they'd be my tutors."

Mom nodded her approval. "Well, that's good!"

"Yeah." I settled back in my chair. "It is, isn't it?"

"So after the quiz, you got in trouble for sneaking into the lab?" asked Dad.

I giggled. "Well, before the lab I got ambushed in a dodgeball game."

Mom raised an eyebrow. "You weren't supposed to be playing."

I raised both my hands defensively. "I wasn't at first! But then a bunch of kids who wanted me to play came after me."

Dad winced. "Must've been a massacre."

"Nope!" I slapped my hand on the table. "We beat them and everyone cheered."

At that, *Dad* cheered but Mom asked, "We?"

"Katie Kestler stepped in at the last minute to help me," I explained. "She's really good at dodgeball."

"Sounds like she's really good at being a friend too," Mom said with a smile.

I swirled the last of the hot cocoa around in my cup. "You know, now that I think about it, today had its bad moments, but overall it was pretty good. I'm lucky to have such great friends and family." I grinned at my parents. "And yes, I mean that."

Mom put her arm around me and hugged me close.

"I didn't even need my good-luck charm," I added teasingly, at which point Mom's fingers tickled my side.

"You keep mentioning that," said Dad while I squirmed and laughed. "How did you even know what you were making was a good-luck charm?"

Reaching down for my bag, I pulled out *Living the Charmed Life*.

"I used this." I opened it to the good-luck charm and turned the book so they could see. "I had the wish circle and the candle . . ." I tapped the page with my finger, and as I did, a strange thing happened. The top part of the page peeled away, revealing another page underneath. "Wait. Huh?"

"The bottom of the page is missing. It looks like you were reading only half of it," said Dad.

"No." I flipped the top of the page out of the

way and saw the rest of my charm on the bottom of the page underneath. But across the top of *that* page was written "For a Great Marriage."

I'd combined instructions for two different charms.

My mouth dropped open. I hadn't made a good-luck charm after all.

"Brooke?" asked Mom.

All those good things that had happened . . . they'd only been lucky because I saw them that way. And all the bad things had only been *un*lucky for the same reason. Which meant . . .

"I really don't have bad luck!" I threw my hands in the air. My spirits soared, and I felt almost giddy with relief. I leaned over and hugged Mom. "I'm not doomed!"

Mom laughed. "I never thought you were."

"The Strikers aren't doomed!" This time I hugged Dad.

"Of course not!" he agreed. "Not with you on the team!"

For some reason, his words brought me back to earth.

I sat in my chair. "Yeah, but being the best on the team still doesn't make our team the best." I made a face. "With Lacey and me out and Kayla gone, the entire front line is different, and if everyone doesn't start playing better, we don't have a chance in this first game. And they all count toward the title."

Dad shrugged. "So help your coach whip them into shape, Captain."

"I will," I said. "But we don't have much time."

"There isn't anyone else you can ask to help?" asked Mom with a meaningful raise of her eyebrow.

"Awww!" I groaned. "Not Lacey. She's the worst!"

"Is she?" asked Dad with an optimistic smile. "Or do you just see her that way?"

"No, she really is quite awful," Mom chimed in.

"Oh." Dad blinked. "Then maybe we should get some more cupcakes to win her over."

CHAPTER

11

No Fate

"This'll only take a few minutes," I promised, getting out of the car. I clutched my coat tighter around me, doing my best not to squish the cupcakes balanced on my splinted arm, and hurried up the steps to ring the doorbell.

A blond guy around my age answered the door, and we frowned at each other.

The last time I'd seen him, he'd been backstabbing one of my friends, and I'd publicly called him out for it.

"Yeah?" he asked.

"Always a delight, Jefferson," I said. "Can I

talk to your sister? I have cupcakes." I held out a pink box.

He clucked his tongue and shook his head. "I'm pretty sure she doesn't want to talk to you. But thanks for the dessert." He grabbed the box from me and started to close the door. I pushed with my whole body so that he stumbled backward. "Dude! What gives?"

"Go. Get. Lacey." I scowled at him, edging my way inside. "The future of the Strikers depends on it."

"Seriously?" Lacey appeared at the entrance to her living room, fuzzy robe over her pajamas and hair disheveled like she'd been sleeping in a wind tunnel. "Don't you think that's a tad overdramatic?"

"Clearly, you haven't seen our replacements play," I said, wrinkling my nose as she pulled a crumpled tissue from the pocket of her robe. Lacey blew her nose and returned the treasure to her pocket. "Are you feeling any better?"

She stared at me with groggy, red eyes. "Do I look like I'm feeling better?"

"Well, you have to hurry this up." I gestured at her whole body. "Because we're going to lose on Saturday if you're not there."

Lacey leaned against the doorframe and crossed her arms. "Really. The amazing Brooke Jacobs finally admits she's not the only good player? I'm shocked."

"I was too," I confessed while Lacey rolled her eyes. "But I realized it doesn't matter how great I play by myself. Soccer is a team sport, and we're only as strong as our weakest link."

"Which right now is me." Lacey pointed to herself. "I'm barely able to stand. If my brother wasn't holding me up—"

"He's not. That's a wall," I corrected.

Lacey blinked in surprise and glanced around. "Where'd he go?"

I knew now wasn't the time for snide remarks, so I continued with my point. "You're not our weakest link, but I need your help dealing with the ones who are." I took a deep breath. "I want you to be my co-captain."

Lacey laughed and then coughed and then hacked something into her tissue. I tried to breathe the air as little as possible.

"I'm not going to be your co-captain!" she told me. "When I start feeling better, I'm going back to showing Coach that he needs to assign a new captain."

I narrowed my eyes. "What do you mean, 'going back to'?"

Lacey's cheeks reddened even more than they were. "If you had a bad day on Monday, I might have had something to do with it."

"You . . . you what?" I stared at her, wide-eyed, and watched her shrink several inches.

"I greased your cleats while you went to the

bathroom," she said in a small voice. "And I gave you a ball I knew was a dud."

I held my hand to my forehead. "Why? I know we don't like each other, but that is seriously low."

Lacey paused for a moment and said, "Brooke, I'm going to tell you something, and if you ever tell anyone I said it, I'll convince everyone you're crazy."

"This is off to a promising start," I said, raising an eyebrow.

"You're pretty good at soccer, all right?" She covered her eyes as if she'd just confessed to something embarrassing, like wearing footie pajamas. "And it makes *me* crazy that you also have a boyfriend and best friends and parents who come to watch you play. I want at least one of those things."

I'd never seen Lacey so vulnerable. It was creeping me out.

"Well . . . thank you," I said. "You're pretty good too. That's why I want you as my co-captain."

It was her turn to look startled. "Still? After I tried to sabotage you? If I were you, I'd be furious."

"Oh, I am," I assured her. "But I can't make this all about me. The team is more important. Now, how soon can you be healthy?"

Lacey smiled weakly. "You think I've got this on my calendar?" She sniffled and shook her head. "I had some tests at the doctor today, so I'll know more tomorrow." Lacey ventured over to the couch and collapsed against the arm.

"Have you been getting lots of rest and taking vitamin C?" I asked.

"If you stick me, I'll bleed Tropicana," she said. "And I've been trapped in bed since Monday night." She pointed at the ceiling. "This is the first trip I've actually made downstairs since I went up after soccer practice that day." She glanced around again. "My mom bought a new lamp."

Jefferson appeared in the doorway, mouth full of cupcake, and mumbled, "You have to leave. Dad says Lacey needs rest."

"I've been resting for three days!" said Lacey, but she got to her feet and gave me a tight smile. "Sorry for everything that happened, and . . . I hope things go better with the team tomorrow. Tell everyone I said hi."

Lacey's brother opened the front door and stood there expectantly.

I nodded to Lacey. "Hopefully you can tell them yourself," I said. Then I left.

"So?" asked Mom when I got back in the car. "How did it go?"

"I'm not sure yet," I confessed. "But I did what I could."

I just hoped Lacey cared enough about the team to consider my offer.

The next morning, Friday, I woke with paws prodding my smiling face.

"Good morning, Chelsea!" I picked her up and lifted her into the air. She splayed her paws and mewed at me until I put her down.

I threw back the covers, hopped out of bed, and changed into my nicest jeans and shirt. V and I had talked after I saw Lacey, and apparently I was the hot gossip in school.

"When you come back tomorrow, all eyes will be on you," she'd told me. "So make it count."

I thundered down the stairs to breakfast, which to my utter joy was delicious, melty cinnamon rolls.

"Yum! Can it be Friday every day?" I asked.

Mom chuckled and slipped a roll onto a plate for me. "Consider these a special treat," she said. "But I'm glad they make you so happy."

"It's not the cinnamon rolls, Mom. It's life!" I

took a deep whiff of sugary heaven.

She handed me a glass of milk and carried her own plate to the table, where Dad was eating a bowl of cereal.

"Does this mean you're ready to face the world, no matter what?" he asked.

"Absolutely." I tore off a piece of sticky pastry and shoved it into my mouth. "Because whatever it brings, I can handle it."

"That's my girl!" he cheered, toasting me with his coffee mug. I clinked my glass of milk against it.

"I'm even ready for the nicknames people might call me after I tried to steal the Bunsen burner," I said.

"Really?" Mom grinned. "Like what?"

"Brooke the Crook, the Bunsen Burglar, Lab Looter . . ."

Mom and Dad were cracking up.

"The Auburn Almost-Arsonist," said Mom with a wink.

Dad pointed at me. "The Red Menace."

I beamed at him. "That would be an awesome soccer nickname!"

When Dad and I stepped outside to head for school, it was snowing. I tilted my head back and let the flakes hit my cheeks, melting into icy dots on my face. I'd seen snow every year since I was a baby, but now I was seeing it differently. It really was all about perspective.

"Snow is amazing," I said. "So fluffy and soft and cold."

"And soaking into your coat," he said. "Let's get in the car."

The entire ride, I gazed out the window and watched the snow flurries whip across the windshield. Dad pulled into the carpool lane, and I jumped out.

"Have a good day!" he called.

"I will!" I shouted, and sprinted into the building, ready to face whatever was coming.

There were some stares when I walked into the student lounge, but mostly people wanted to know why I'd broken into the lab. I made it roughly five steps before the questions started.

"I wanted to try a science experiment on my own" was all I told them.

"Did you really get suspended?" asked Tim's sister, Gabby.

"Of course she didn't. She's here, isn't she?"

"Actually, I got suspended for the afternoon," I confessed. "It was super embarrassing."

"Oh my God, I would *die* if I got suspended," said Katie. "Mainly because my parents would kill me."

Several people laughed, and in the distance I heard my name being called. I stood on my tiptoes and saw Vanessa and Heather waving to me from a couch. I said good-bye to the kids around me and hurried to join my friends.

"Thank goodness you're okay!" said Heather, hugging me.

I laughed. "Of course I'm okay. You saw me in the principal's office, remember?"

"Yes, but I've had that hug waiting since then."

All three of us laughed, and I sat between my friends on the couch.

"Guys, I've got to tell you something serious," I said. "Actually, Tim should probably hear this too." I glanced around the student lounge and saw him talking to a couple of girls. "Tim!" I bellowed.

He jumped and turned toward us before saying something to the girls and running over.

"What's up, Foghorn?" he asked.

I looked to all three of my friends. "I wasn't cursed with bad luck, and that wasn't a real good-luck charm I had."

Vanessa gasped and clutched at her chest. "No way! You mean all this time . . . I was right?" She relaxed and grinned at me.

"Ha-ha," I said.

"What made you change your mind?" asked Heather.

"I did a lot of soul-searching yesterday afternoon," I said with a sage nod. "And thinking about what's really important." I cleared my throat. "Also, it turned out I was making a marriage charm."

My friends looked at one another and doubled over laughing.

"Hey, listen." Tim cupped his hand around his ear. "You can almost hear Abel screaming and running for the exit."

"Be nice!" I said, pushing him. "You realize if my situation wasn't real, it means you won't be a millionaire by Monday either."

He waved me off. "Yeah, I gave up on that when the next step to fortune and glory was sending the author fifty bucks for the next book in the series."

I made a face. "Sorry." I turned to Heather. "And I'm sorry I messed up your date with Emmett."

"It's okay," she said with a smile. "He and I talked, and since we don't see eye to eye on dating, we agreed that we're better off as friends."

"Aw." I leaned forward and hugged her. Then I turned to V and hugged *her*.

"Not that I don't appreciate it, but what was that for?" she asked.

"For putting up with me even when I was being a bit of a dork," I said.

"You mean a huge dork," she corrected me, laughing. "And I'm your best friend. I'm always going to be there for you."

"Me too!" said Heather.

The three of us hugged, and Tim shifted his weight from side to side. "Are we done here? Because if I don't get back to those girls I was talking to, *I'm* going to have bad luck."

"Almost," I said. "Has Mrs. H changed her mind about letting us enter the newspaper contest?" I asked.

Tim shook his head.

"Nope," said V.

Heather sighed. "This morning I saw Mary Patrick dunking a king-size Hershey bar in a jar of peanut butter."

I nodded. "That's what I figured. Which is why I came up with this." I pulled a sheet of paper out of my notebook.

"What is it?" asked Tim, taking it from me.

"It's an agreement for everyone on the newspaper staff to sign," I said. "It says if *any* section wins an award, they have to split the money with the rest of the newspaper staff."

"'Because when one of us wins, we all win,'" Heather read from the agreement. "I like it!" She took the paper from Tim and signed the top line.

"But whichever section wins will still gloat about it," said Vanessa. "And Mrs. H won't like that."

"Which is why there's a line in the agreement about *that*." I pointed. "'Good sportsmanship means being gracious in victory or defeat. We will be both.'"

"Here's hoping this works," said V, adding her name below Heather's.

I signed below them and passed the paper back to Tim, who sighed.

"You know sharing money is against everything I stand for," he said, scrawling his name on the page.

The bell rang, and there was a general shuffle of movement toward the door.

"And now to track the other members down

in homeroom and get the rest of the signatures," I said.

"Hurry," said Heather. "You don't want to be in trouble two days in a row."

I pointed at my feet and winked. "That's why I got my good sneakers on."

I pushed through the crowd and sprinted for the eighth-grade hall.

Getting signatures ended up taking all the way through lunch, but everyone was eager to sign. When I snuck the list to Mary Patrick at the start of Journalism, she put down her jar of peanut butter and gave me an actual, real-life hug.

"Was that like hugging a robot?" asked Tim as I sat down.

"Actually, it was more like hugging a five-year-old," I said, feeling my hair. "I think she got a piece of candy bar stuck in here."

For once, the entire classroom was quiet when Mrs. H walked in, and when Mary Patrick handed her the *Lincoln Log* agreement, she read it with tears in her eyes.

"I couldn't be more proud," said Mrs. H, clutching the paper to her chest, "to be the adviser who shares in your victory."

The entire class cheered, and instantly Mary Patrick was back in action.

"Okay, I've made a few tweaks to the paper based on suggestions from our team leaders." She turned on the projector, and Mrs. H smiled.

"That fast, huh?"

Mary Patrick smiled sheepishly. "I was kind of hoping you'd change your mind."

An image of the front page appeared on the dry-erase board.

"You'll notice we've changed the look a bit," said Mary Patrick. "Along the right border, we've got shaded squares positioned at different heights based on what section of the paper it is."

I sat up a little taller and puffed out my chest.

That had been one of my ideas, based on V's cloth tabs for different clothing designs.

"We've also bolded key words, like dates, places, and people, so readers can focus on what's important about each piece."

Also my idea! Heather wanted to be bold and stand out, and so would our newspaper.

Mary Patrick continued to go through the changes, all of which I had to say were impressive, including my third idea, which I'd based off Tim's constant want for money.

"We're doing a classifieds section?" someone asked. "Cool! It's like a real paper!"

When we broke into our small groups, I told my friends which suggestions I'd made, and they all smiled proudly. Before class ended, Gil wandered over to our team with something behind his back and a big smile on his face.

"Ooh! Do you have a present for me?" asked Vanessa, trying to peek behind him.

"For the paper, actually," he said, revealing what he'd been hiding.

It was a photo taken during my PE class the day before, where Katie and I had faced off against eleven kids in dodgeball . . . and emerged victorious.

Heather, Vanessa, and Tim all cheered, and I clapped a hand over my mouth.

"I thought it perfectly summed up beating the odds," said Gil. "But I didn't want to submit it without Brooke's permission." He gave me a hopeful smile, and I nodded.

"It's perfect. Go for it."

Considering how horribly the week had started, it was actually turning out to be pretty good. I made a few last-minute tweaks to my response to Swimfan, based on my own personal experiences, and when I turned in my team's advice to Mrs. H, she gave me a knowing smile.

"Thanks for all your hard work," she said,

and I knew she was talking about more than the advice column.

That afternoon when I got to the soccer complex, I made a beeline for the locker room to see if Lacey was there. She wasn't.

"Has anyone heard from Lacey?" I asked the other girls who were changing.

"I think she's still sick," someone said.

"Oh," I said, checking my watch. "Well, I'm sure we'll be okay without her."

"You said you were going to come up with ways to help us," said Brin. "Did you?"

I nodded. "I've got some videos for you, Lana, and Allison to watch that'll help with the areas where you're having trouble. For Jenny too. And I came up with a couple drills to help."

"Neat!" she said. "What else?"

I hesitated. "What else?"

I didn't have anything else. I'd been so busy

trying to get the newspaper back in the contest and finding videos that I hadn't thought of anything else.

Then a voice spoke from the doorway. A stuffy, snotty voice. "We need to talk to Coach about running plays that work toward your strengths," said Lacey.

"You came!" I cried, walking over to her. "Can you play?"

Lacey shook her head. "The doctor says it's not pneumonia, but he doesn't want me playing until next week," she said. "So I'm just here to help with training . . ." She paused and added, "As your co-captain."

"Great! Let's go tell Coach." I nudged her out the locker room exit.

As soon as we were out of earshot of the others, she said, "You know we're not friends."

"I know." I stopped and turned to face her,

grinning. "But we're also not enemies."

Lacey rolled her eyes and smirked. "Just keep walking, Brooke."

"Actually," I said, "it's the Red Menace."

Dear Swimfan,

Being a top athlete takes physical and mental training. You're not alone when you say you crack under pressure and lose your talent. Athletes even have a term for it: choking. But it's important to remember that the fear is in your head. Which means you can get rid of it! Sometimes we're our own worst enemies, and we don't succeed because we tell ourselves we can't. Tell yourself you CAN and watch what happens. (But keep your eyes closed underwater, because chlorine stings.) I believe in you!

Confidentially yours,
Brooke Jacobs

Acknowledgments

Always for family, friends, and God.

For the new members of my family, because they make my heart even bigger.

For Eve Mercado, who I hope grows up to be an awesome reader.

For my brother-in-law Will, because he works hard, sacrifices much, and puts up with my sister.

For Paul Blackthorne, the person I envisioned when I wrote Coach Bly. Thanks for the inspiration!

And for the SCBWI, who encourage writers and illustrators to dream and do big things.

Turn the page for a sneak peek at the next book
in the Confidentially Yours series:

CHAPTER

1

Unconfidentially Yours

"**M**ajor disaster! End of the world!" Katie Kestler sprinted toward me, waving her hands over her head.

I lifted an eyebrow but didn't join the panic. . . . Mostly because it's not my style, but also because I'd recently bought a cute sweater. The world wasn't allowed to end until I'd worn it at least twice.

"What's going on?" I asked.

"And how can you run in those shoes?" added Tim Antonides, peering at Katie's heeled boots.

He was sitting beside me at lunch, along with

my other best friends Brooke Jacobs and Heather Schwartz.

"I actually can't." Katie's panicked expression turned into a pained one, and she dropped into a nearby chair. As she bent to inspect one of her boots, she placed a fabric scrap on our table.

Brooke picked it up.

"I'm guessing the major disaster has to do with this red cloth," she said. "That, or you've started miniature bullfighting."

"No, you had it right the first time," Katie said, straightening. "The cloth is the wrong shade of red. Vanessa and I ordered crimson." She took the swatch from Brooke and held it up for my inspection.

"Oh no. Poppy?" I clapped a hand to my forehead. "What happened to *our* fabric?"

Katie and I are the future of fashion. When she moved in across the street a few months ago, we started talking clothes, and not before too long we'd come up with our own company: KV Fashions.

Lately, we'd been stocking material so we could sew tops for a runway show we were holding at Abraham Lincoln Middle School. It hadn't been easy to get approval to use the stage, but luckily, Katie's parents were good friends with the principal, and we'd promised all the money from ticket sales would go to improving the campus. Plus, Katie pointed out that our success could also be good for the school.

That was, of course, before the Great Crimson Crisis.

"The fabric company ran out of our color and thought we'd settle for this!" Katie threw the swatch down in disgust, and it landed on top of Tim's mac 'n' cheese. He calmly used it to wipe the corner of his mouth and then kept eating.

"Maybe you can find the red you want at a fabric store in town," suggested Heather.

I shook my head. "We already looked. The closest match Dee's Fabric World had was cherry, which was a little dark, and ketchup, which was a little ugly."

Heather and Brooke laughed.

I shrugged at Katie. "We're just gonna have to make the poppy work. Who knows? Maybe it'll look better than the crimson."

Katie leaned over and put a hand on mine. "You are so brave, Vanny."

Tim nudged Brooke. "Did the meaning of that word change while I was in the lunch line?"

"I wouldn't say 'brave,'" I told Katie while I pinched Tim's arm. "Just optimistic."

She nodded and stood, pulling her phone out of her back pocket. "Excuse me. I have to call my mom, my dad, and my life coach."

"I can't believe you guys are still waiting for fabric to come in," said Brooke as Katie hurried away. "If I were you—"

"You wouldn't be wearing sweatpants right now?" I asked with an innocent smile.

Brooke lifted one of her legs. "These are comfy *and* functional, which is exactly what I told Abel when he called me Lazy McSweatpants this morning." She lowered her leg and narrowed her eyes. "Did he tell you to mock them?"

Abel Hart was her seventh-grade boyfriend who loved to tease her almost as much as I did. Brooke would've worn gym shorts to the school dance if that was an option.

"Abel didn't need to tell me. Those things demand to be judged," I said.

Brooke stuck her tongue out at me. "What I was *going* to say was that if I were you, I would've already had all the clothes sewn and on hangers by now."

"Ha!" said Tim. "This from the girl who's usually the last to turn in her assignment for the paper?"

Brooke, Heather, Tim, and I write an advice column, "Lincoln's Letters," for our school's newspaper, the *Lincoln Log*. And despite the fact that Brooke is our section leader, she definitely doesn't set the best example.

Brooke raised her eyebrow and countered, "This from the guy who's usually the last to show up for class?"

Heather waved the scrap of cloth between them. "Break it up, you two! Truce!"

"Technically, a red flag is a symbol for battle," said Tim, "so you're actually telling us to go for it. Unless you're color-blind and think that's white." He gestured at the fabric.

Heather narrowed her eyes in mock disapproval. "Do you want to see even more red? Because I can make that happen."

"Ooh!" said Brooke and I.

Tim grinned and leaned back, holding up his hands. "Okay, okay! I've never seen your dark side before, and I'm kind of scared of it."

I laughed. "Does Heather even *have* a dark side?"

Brooke leaned forward and spoke in a whisper. "I'll bet it involves texting in all caps. And *not* saying thank you!"

The rest of us laughed, including Heather. Of our group, she was the most level-headed person, and more likely to stop a fight than start one.

"Hey, I can be tough when I need to be," she assured us. "Just tell me I can only have one serving at an all-you-can-eat buffet and watch the meat loaf fly."

"Flying meat loaf." Brooke shuddered. "That stuff's scary enough when it's just sitting on a plate."

We all laughed again.

"Anyway, to get back to what you were saying earlier," I told Brooke, "I'll have you know it takes me two days to make a top *with* embellishments.

I only need seven for this show, and I've already made three. Two weeks is plenty of time to find my models, sew the rest of my shirts, and have the fittings."

"Pfft. Models," Brooke scoffed. "So lame."

"Really? I was hoping you'd be one."

"I'd love to!" she beamed, and I rolled my eyes.

"As long as what I wear is dignified," she added.

"Too late," I said. "You're wearing a donkey costume with Tim."

"Dibs on the front end!" he said.

I turned to Heather. "I know you're not a huge fan of being singled out, but would you consider at least wearing one look down the runway? For me?" I pressed my hands together and gave her a pleading pout.

Heather smiled. "If it's for you, I think I can make an exception."

I reached over and squeezed her. "Yay!"

"Do you need help finding the rest of the models?" asked Tim. "Because I would be willing to sacrifice my time for the search." He put on his most solemn expression.

I narrowed my eyes. "If I didn't know you so well, I'd *almost* think you were offering to help me and not yourself."

"It's been a slow winter in the dating world," he confessed.

"Has it been a slow winter?" Brooke tilted her head. "Or have girls finally written enough bad things about you in Locker 411?"

"Ooh!" Heather and I said.

Tim pointed at Brooke. "That is also entirely possible."

Locker 411 was something Tim's twin sister, Gabby, created as an info source for all students. Kids can post in the different topic binders with gossip and announcements.

"Speaking of which," I said, "that's actually

where we put our sign-up sheet for our model search. It's really been filling up." I beamed. "We've got about fifteen people to choose from so far."

"And we're about to have more!" Katie rushed back toward the table, this time in striped socks, with her phone and boots in hand. "You'll never guess what my mom just told me!"

"Running in heels is a bad idea?" asked Brooke.

Katie hesitated. "You'll never guess what *else* my mom just told me!" Instead of waiting for more guesses, she plowed ahead. "My dad knows a buyer at a local boutique, and she's going to sit in on our fashion show. If she likes what she sees, our designs could be on the rack by summer!"

Instantly, I was out of my seat. "Are you serious?"

Katie nodded. "Serious as the pain shooting up my legs!"

I squealed and hugged her, bouncing up and down. She squealed too, but followed it with, "Vanny, you're jumping on my foot!"

"Sorry, I'm just so excited!" I backed away and clutched my hands to my chest. "We could be in a *boutique!*" I turned to my other friends, and they smiled.

"That's awesome!" agreed Brooke.

"So proud of you!" said Heather.

"Very cool. Which store?" asked Tim.

"Lazenby's," said Katie.

"Ooh! I love that place," said Heather. "And now I love it even more!"

"Lazenby's?" I asked. "Wow, I haven't shopped there in ages."

It was in an older shopping center near the edge of town, which made it too far to go alone. And if Mom had to drive, I'd rather she take me into Chicago where there were loads more options.

"Hey, money is money," said Tim. "If you don't want it, I'll take it."

He's been on a get-rich-quick kick since he became best friends with Berkeley Dennis, whose parents are billionaires or something.

Tim did have a point, though. I glanced up at the cafeteria clock and faced Katie. "We have fifteen minutes before I have to get to Journalism. I think it's time to pay a visit to Locker 411 and fix our flyer. Shall we?"

"We shall!" She made a sweeping gesture down the hall. "But walk ahead of me, because I have to put my boots back on, and I may need you to break my fall if I stumble."

"Heh. That's the first time I've heard someone else say that and not me," I commented.

I waved to the rest of my friends and walked with Katie to Locker 411. The inner walls of the locker were lined with notes about upcoming fund-raisers and the latest gossip, but our model audition sign-up sheet had been taped on the inside of the door. At first, I'd been worried people would doodle all over the stock photos of models that decorated the sheet, but so far only one of the pictures had a mustache.

"Should we take this down and put up a new flyer or—"

I stopped as something taped beside our ad caught my eye.

It was a clipping from the previous week's advice column of a question from an anonymous reader who went by the name Wigging Out.

Dear Lincoln's Letters,

My hair is really thin, so I've been pretty much bald my whole life. And I'm a girl. This means I wear a wig to school. Nobody's figured out that it's not my real hair yet, but I'm getting tired of the same style and color. Do you think anyone would notice if I changed wigs?

Since I was in charge of giving fashion and beauty advice for the column, I'd answered the question, but someone had scribbled over my words with a black marker:

Who is Wigging Out? Put your guess below.

People were trying to figure out who this poor girl without any hair was?

Beneath that were two names, the top one scribbled in pencil and the other in blue ink.

The one in pencil said *Katie Kestler.*

My jaw dropped.